Root and Thorn

The Warden-Apprentice and the Saundered War

Robin Parker

2026

Table of Contents

ISBN (Hardback):978-1-7644912-5-9

ISBN (Paperback): 978-1-7644912-2-8

ISBN (eBook):978-1-7644912-3-5

Library of Congress Control Number: 2026905867

Published by Robin Parker

Sarasotas, Florida, USA

First Edition

Author's Note

Growing up doesn't always mean having choices.

Sometimes it means dealing with situations you didn't
ask for and can't change right away.

We can't always control where we are, what happens to
us, or what other people do. That can feel unfair,
frustrating, or even overwhelming. But there is one thing
we do have control over: how we react.

This story is about growth - not the kind that happens
all at once, but the kind that happens slowly, while you're
still figuring things out. It's for anyone who has ever felt
stuck and wondered if things could be different someday.

They can.

CHAPTER 1: A Different World

The cottage appeared at the end of the lane like something from a storybook, and Anna, pressed against the car window, felt her stomach tighten. The last few hours of driving had given her too much time to think about the raised voices behind closed doors, about her mother pretending everything was fine at breakfast, about the way neither parent would quite look at each other anymore. Or at her.

The cottage had walls of honey-coloured stone that rose to a proper first floor beneath a roof thick with moss, soft and green as velvet. Roses gone wild clambered over the front door, their blooms heavy with rain. It didn't look like a house that worried about anything at all.

"Here we are," her father said, his voice too cheerful. "Aunt Jacqueline's."

Anna clutched her backpack and watched the car roll to a stop. The engine died, and suddenly the only sound was birdsong and the distant bleating of sheep. Her father got out, walked around, and opened her door for her, something he hadn't done since she was very small.

She slid out, the weight of the last few months sitting on her small shoulders like a heavy, invisible coat. The whispered arguments, the strained silence, the final, tearful decision that she should stay here for a while.

The cottage door burst open before either of them could speak.

"You're here!" The woman who emerged was a whirlwind of colour and warmth. Aunt Jacqueline was nothing like Anna's mother. Where Anna's mum was neat and tidy, Aunt Jacqueline was ... overflowing. Her hair, streaked with grey, escaped a messy bun in frizzy tendrils. She wore a paint-splattered smock over a pair of men's corduroy trousers, and her smile was so wide and genuine it seemed to light up the damp afternoon.

"Well, hello, stranger," she said to Anna's dad, pulling him into a brief, firm hug. Then her bright green eyes, the same shade as Anna's mother's, settled on Anna.

"My goodness," Aunt Jacqueline breathed. "Look at you."

There was a pause, just a beat of awkwardness where no one quite knew what to do next. Anna shifted her weight from foot to foot.

"I should ..." her father started, glancing at his watch. "I've got to get back to London. It's a long way, and I don't like leaving your mum worrying."

He knelt, pulling Anna into a hug that smelled of car seats and old worries. It was tight and warm, and Anna squeezed back, burying her face in his shoulder for one long moment.

"You be good," he murmured into her hair. "Write to us, yeah? We'll call. Soon." He pulled back, his eyes glistening. He gave her a wobbly smile, ruffled her hair, and climbed back into the car without another word.

Anna stood watching as the car reversed down the lane, a shrinking grey shape until it vanished around the bend. The silence that followed was vast and heavy.

And then Aunt Jacqueline's arms were around her, sweeping her into a hug that smelled of earth, herbs, and woodsmoke.

It was bigger than her father's hug, somehow warmer, as if it came from a deeper place.

"Oh, let me look at you!" Her aunt held her at arm's length, her eyes missing nothing. "All grown up and so serious! And look how you've grown, the last time I saw you, you were knee-high and chasing butterflies with a jam jar. You must have been... what, five?"

Anna nodded vaguely. She had no memory of that visit, only a faint impression of a sunny garden and the smell of cut grass. It felt like a story about someone else.

"Well, we'll have to fix that," Aunt Jacqueline said, her smile softening. She kept one arm around Anna's shoulders as she steered her toward the door. "Come in, come in, you must be frozen!"

The cottage interior was a glorious, organised chaos. Every surface held something fascinating: a bowl of speckled eggs, a stack of leather-bound books, a half-carved piece of wood that was becoming an owl. Dried flowers hung from the beams, and the air was thick with the scent of drying lavender and something baking. On the wall by the stove hung a beautiful, slightly strange painting of a fairy with fierce eyes and hair of vibrant pink streaked with bold, emerald green.

Anna stared at it.

Aunt Jacqueline followed her gaze. "Ah, you like her? A local artist. Sees things the rest of us don't." She winked, a quick flash that could have meant anything or nothing at all. "More tea?"

As her aunt bustled back to the stove, humming a tune that sounded like wind through reeds, Anna's eyes continued their inventory. A mobile of crow feathers and delicate, pearlescent bones turned slowly above the sink, though no window was open. On the deep windowsill, a row of homemade ceramic jars held not pencils or flour, but pebbles, feathers, and pods that clicked softly in the draft. One jar, stoppered with a cork, held what looked like glittering sand. Anna squinted. It seemed to be moving, ever so slightly, like it was breathing.

This wasn't just a different house. It was a different planet.

"Right then," Aunt Jacqueline said, clapping her flour-dusted hands. "Let's get you settled. Your room's a bit of a 'creative space', mind. I hope you don't mind sharing quarters with a few dormant projects."

She led Anna up a narrow staircase that creaked a friendly greeting with each step. The room at the top was, as promised, small. It was clearly the former headquarters of every craft Aunt Jacqueline had ever flirted with. A beautiful, ancient sewing machine sat under a slope of the ceiling like a sleeping metal beetle. Shelves were crammed with mason jars containing buttons, dried lavender heads, bundles of twigs tied with red string, and balls of yarn in colours with names like "Storm Cloud" and "Dragon's Blood."

But in the midst of the creative chaos, a space had been carved out for her. A single bed was pushed against the wall, heaped with a quilt that was a mosaic of a hundred different fabrics and velvets, faded florals, rough tartans. It felt like a hug. A small, wobbly-looking desk held a brand-new notebook, its pages blank and promising, and a cup of sharpened pencils. The window looked out not onto a street or another house, but onto a tangle of green and colour so vibrant it looked like a painting.

"It's perfect," Anna said, and she meant it. The room didn't feel temporary. It felt like a cocoon, a secret den where a new kind of thinking might happen.

"Good," her aunt said, her voice softening. "Make it yours. The garden's yours to explore, too. Just ... be back before the light goes all watery. The woods have a different personality at dusk." Again, that glint in her eye. A statement that was also a gentle, mysterious warning.

The moment the door clicked shut, the quiet of the cottage wrapped around Anna. It was a living quiet, full of ticks and sighs and the distant buzz of insects. The pull from the window was magnetic. After the long journey, the painful goodbye, and the weight of the unknown, her limbs itched with the need to move, to see, to not think about the deep worry lines on her father's forehead or the forced cheer in her mother's voice.

She didn't bother to unpack. She simply turned, walked back down the singing stairs, and let herself out the sun-warped back door.

The scent hit her first, an explosion of damp soil, sweet peas, rosemary, and something richer, like crushed green leaves and warm stone. It was the smell of life, unchecked and generous. Aunt Jacqueline's garden wasn't arranged in neat rows, it was a joyful riot. Sunflowers stood as tall as guardsmen beside frothy clouds of Queen Anne's Lace. Strawberries spilled from raised beds, and fat bumblebees bobbed between foxgloves that stood like purple spires.

And at the bottom of the garden, just a few strides beyond a
rustic arch woven with honeysuckle, stood the dark, dense
line of the woods.

Anna took a deep breath, the kind that fills you up to your
fingertips. For the first time in months, the knot in her chest
loosened. She took a step off the flagstone path, her shoe
sinking into the soft, cool grass, and began to explore.

The garden did not give up its secrets all at once. It offered
them, one by one, like precious stones placed softly in Anna's
palm. She spent the rest of the afternoon in a state of quiet,
mesmerised exploration. She left the flagstone path behind,
her shoes soon dusted with rich, dark soil. She ran her
fingers over the velvety fur of a lamb's ear leaf, startling at its
softness. She followed the industrious journey of a ladybug
across a broad rhubarb leaf. She found a corner where
snapdragons grew in a riot of crimson and gold, and when
she gently squeezed their sides, the blooms opened like tiny,
satisfied mouths.

The sheer aliveness of it was a tonic. This wasn't the
managed, distant green of a city park. This was a thriving,
humming, pushing, blooming entity.

Bees, fat and dusted with pollen, worked with a purpose that
felt important. The air itself was a shifting tapestry of scent:
one moment the sharp, clean perfume of rosemary, the next
the honeyed sigh of the honeysuckle arch.

Eventually, drawn by a particularly lush patch of clover and
chamomile near the strawberry beds, Anna simply lay down.
The earth beneath her was cool and firm, cradling her spine.

She looked up, and the world became a frame of green stalks and colourful petals against an endless, slow-drifting sky. Clouds, white and ponderous, became sailing ships, sleeping dragons, castles made of mist.

Here, with the scent of warm earth in her nose and the gentle buzz of life in her ears, the tight knot of worry finally, completely, unravelled. The goodbyes, the silent car ride, the unspoken fear in her parents' eyes, all of it faded. She wasn't a girl in a strange place. She was a girl who had, by some miracle, come home to a place she'd never known she belonged.

She was so far adrift in this blissful, imaginary world that her aunt's call from the back door seemed to come from a great distance.

"Anna! Dusk-thief is coming! Time to come in."

Anna sat up, blinking. The light had changed. It had gone golden and thick, slanting long shadows across the garden. The flowers seemed to glow from within. With a deep, contented sigh, she brushed off her clothes and went inside.

The kitchen was a haven of warmth and tantalising smells. A simple ceramic dish sat in the centre of the wooden table, steaming. It was a medley of roasted vegetables, chunks of golden potato, caramelised carrots, glistening peppers, and meaty-looking mushrooms, all glazed with a dark, fragrant sauce and sprinkled with fresh herbs.

"I hope you're hungry," Aunt Jacqueline said, placing a hunk of crusty bread beside each bowl. "It's all from the garden. Well, except the flour and oil. The fairies haven't started baking for me yet." She said it so offhandedly, with such a twinkle, that it could only be a joke. Couldn't it?

Anna, who usually eyed unknown vegetables with suspicion, took a tentative bite. Her eyes widened. It was delicious. The mushrooms were earthy and rich, the carrots sweet, the potatoes perfectly salted. And there was something else... a faint, elusive whisper on her tongue. A hint of wild garlic, perhaps, or the memory of the flowers she'd been lying amongst.

"It's amazing," Anna said, and she meant it. She ate with a hunger she hadn't felt in weeks.

Between bites, the questions tumbled out. "What's that spiky purple flower by the fence? How do the sunflowers get so tall? Do the bees ever get angry? Where does the little path behind the compost lead?"

Aunt Jacqueline listened, a soft smile playing on her lips. She answered each one, her answers practical yet sprinkled with odd, personal asides.

"That's a globe thistle. The bees adore it, and so do the fairies for its fuzz." Fairies again. "The sunflowers? They listen to a lot of good gossip from the blackbirds, keeps them growing to hear more." "The bees are only cross if you're mean to the flowers. That path? Oh, that just wanders. Sometimes it leads you where you need to go."

Finally, as they were washing up, Anna leaned against the sink, gazing out at the garden now swallowed by twilight. "It's the most beautiful place I've ever seen."

Her aunt came to stand beside her, drying a bowl with a checkered cloth. She looked at Anna, her expression softening into something profound and knowing.

She didn't speak of Anna's parents, or the trouble, or the unspoken reason for this stay. She simply placed a warm, dry hand on Anna's head, her touch smelling of soil and soap.

"You really love it, don't you?" Aunt Jacqueline said, her voice a gentle rumble in the quiet kitchen. "I can see it in your eyes. You're not just looking, you're seeing."

Anna nodded, unable to put the feeling into words.

Her aunt's smile deepened, crinkling the corners of her eyes. "Good," she said, as if sealing a pact. "I think you're going to enjoy it here."

After the last dish was dried and put away, the true quiet of the cottage settled in. Anna noticed it then, the absence of a familiar hum. There was no grey glow of a television in the corner, no murmur of a radio news bulletin. Instead, the evening's soundtrack was the crackle of the stove cooling, the soft tick-tock of a grandfather clock in the hall, and the gentle rustle of leaves against the windowpane.

"I'm afraid I'm not much for modern entertainment," Aunt Jacqueline said, following Anna's gaze around the room. "But I've got plenty of the old-fashioned kind." She gestured to a shelf of books, some with faded gold lettering, others with colourful, peeling dust jackets depicting knights and forests. "Help yourself to any of them. They don't bite," her aunt said with a wink before heading up the stairs, her footsteps a comforting creak on the old wood.

Up in her little room, Anna began the slow process of unpacking. She folded her clothes into the waiting chest of drawers, the familiar textures of home feeling slightly out of place amidst the jars of feathers and balls of wild-coloured yarn. As she placed her hairbrush on the wobbly desk, her eye was caught by a small, particularly shabby book sitting on the shelf just above it.

It was tucked between a thick botany guide and a ledger filled with pressed flowers. Unlike the others, it had no title on its spine. Curious, Anna pulled it free. A little cloud of dust motes danced in the last of the evening light. The cover was of soft, worn green cloth, embossed with a faint, intricate pattern of vines and she peered closer, tiny, winged silhouettes.

Fairies: Myths and Misconceptions of the British Isles was written in elegant, looping script on the title page. The publication date was 1898. Anna's heart gave a little skip. She crawled onto her patchwork quilt, propped herself against the cool wall, and opened the brittle pages.

It was not a storybook. It was a serious-looking, if wildly fanciful, scholarly work. Chapters had titles like "On the Classification of Pixie, Sprite, and Fay" and "The Etiquette of Offering Cream and Bread." There were intricate, hand-drawn illustrations: a regal fairy queen seated on a mushroom throne, a mischievous-looking creature with a pointed hat winking from a foxglove bell, a warning diagram of a "Fairy Ring" of mushrooms, captioned "Do Not Enter, Lest You Be Lost to Time."

Anna read, utterly engrossed. It was all so precise, so certain. The book spoke of fairy gratitude and fairy wrath with equal gravity. It described their love of music, their distaste for iron, their hidden kingdoms in mounds and hollow hills. One passage, underlined in faint brown ink, sent a shiver down her spine:

"To those with the Sight, the Glamour may part. The mortal may step through the veil, but the veil, once pierced, can never again be whole for them."

Outside, the last of the light faded, painting her room in deep blues and purples. The words began to swim on the page. The long journey, the rich food, the overwhelming sensations of the day, all settled upon her like a heavy, warm blanket.

The book slipped from her fingers, coming to rest open on a beautiful, full-page illustration of a wooded glen lit by countless tiny, floating lights.

She didn't remember falling asleep.

Chapter 2: The Rhythm of Green Things

The morning after her arrival, Anna woke not to an alarm, but to a chorus of birdsong so loud and joyous it sounded like a celebration. Sunlight streamed through her new bedroom window, painting a bright rectangle on the floorboards. And winding up through the birds' symphony was the most delicious smell imaginable: the warm, yeasty, utterly comforting scent of fresh bread baking.

For a moment, she was confused by the patchwork quilt, the jars of feathers, the golden light. Then memory flooded back: the garden, the quiet cottage, the strange and wonderful book that now lay beside her on the quilt. She glanced down. It was still open to the beautiful, full-page illustration of a wooded glen lit by countless tiny, floating lights.

Downstairs, something clattered, and her aunt's off-key humming drifted up the stairs.

A new day in a different world had begun.

The smell of bread was even better in the kitchen. It was a warm, solid presence in the air. Aunt Jacqueline set a loaf on the table, its crust golden and crackled, alongside a dish of pale yellow butter and a jar of jam so dark red it was almost purple.

"Blackberry and apple," her aunt said, seeing Anna look at it. "From last autumn's bounty. The fairies love the blackberry brambles. Terrible gossips, brambles." She said it as matter-of-factly as someone else might comment on the weather.

Over breakfast, the bread still warm, the butter melting into its honeycombed holes, Aunt Jacqueline laid out the gentle architecture of Anna's days.

"Now then, while you're with me, there are a few rules of the house," she began, not sternly, but with a practical air. "Your room is for you to keep tidy, I'm not one for fussing, but a clear space makes for a clear mind. You'll give me a hand in the garden when I need it. Nothing too taxing. Mostly, you'll be my second pair of eyes. The beans, for instance, always think they can hide from me."

Anna nodded, her mouth full of the most delicious bread she'd ever tasted.

"As for schoolwork," Aunt Jacqueline continued, pouring them both more tea from a stout brown pot, "your mother and I agreed we'd wait and see. The summer holidays have only just begun, and we don't yet know if you'll be going back home or... settling here a while longer. If it comes to it, there's a small school in the village. One teacher, six children. Very different from what you're used to."

The mention of home, of the uncertain future, cast a tiny, brief shadow. Anna focused on the jam, spreading it carefully.

"But for now," her aunt's voice softened, brightening, "your only assignment is to explore. To read. To follow your nose and your curiosity. The world out there," she gestured with her butter knife towards the sunlit garden, "is the best teacher I know. Just be back when I call you, and don't go into the deep woods after the light turns thick. Deal?"

"Deal," Anna said, the shadow lifting as quickly as it had
come. It sounded like a perfect deal.

After breakfast, Anna helped clear the plates, then followed
her aunt outside with a woven basket. The morning was fresh
and new, every leaf beaded with dew that glittered like
scattered diamonds.

"Right," Aunt Jacqueline said, standing at the edge of the
vegetable patch with the stance of a general surveying her
troops. "This is the heart of the operation. And every heart
has its own rhythm."

What followed was less a gardening lesson and more an
introduction to a society of silent, green beings. Aunt
Jacqueline spoke of the plants not as things, but as
personalities.

"The lettuces," she said, gently touching a frilly green head,
"are shy morning folk. You pick them crisp with the dew on
them, or they sulk and wilt by lunchtime." She
demonstrated, using a small knife to make a clean cut at the
base.

She moved to a row of fat, purple-veined beetroots. "These
are evening souls. They soak up the whole day's sun, and
only give up their sweetness as the light fades. See how the
leaves are perky now? They're still listening to the dawn
chorus. We'll visit them later."

She pointed to a tangle of pea vines heavy with pods. "These
will tell you when they're ready. Not just by feel. Look." She
cradled a plump pod. "See how it curves with pride? Like it's
showing off its treasures. And smell." She snapped the pod

open with her thumb. A scent of incredible, sugary greenness filled the air. "That's their invitation."

Anna listened, fascinated. Her aunt wasn't just reciting gardening tips, she was describing a world of silent communication, of paying attention to details most people would miss.

"The rosemary likes its feet dry and its head in the sun. The mint is a cheerful bully, it will take over if you let it.. The carrots sing to the worms, you know, to keep the soil soft." She handed Anna a pair of scissors. "Here, the basil is asking to be picked. See how the top leaves are big and proud? If we take a few, it will grow bushier, happier. It's an offering, not a theft."

Anna carefully snipped a few fragrant stems, the scent exploding around her fingers. She wasn't sure if her aunt was teasing her, weaving a beautiful story to make gardening fun. She remembered a phrase her parents had used once, quietly, about an eccentric old neighbour: 'Not quite the full quid.' But as she watched Aunt Jacqueline hum to a courgette plant while checking its leaves, her movements fluid and respectful, Anna knew it wasn't that.

This wasn't a lack of something. It was the presence of something else entirely. A deep, quiet knowing. A different way of seeing.

As they carried the basket of sun-warmed vegetables back to the kitchen, Anna stole a glance at her aunt's profile, at the easy smile on her face as she greeted a bumblebee lumbering past. She felt a swell of affection, and something more: a dawning recognition. Her aunt was special. Not in a loud, showy way, but in a way that was rooted and real, like the ancient oak at the bottom of the garden. She saw the world alive, and in doing so, she made Anna feel more alive in it.

"Thank you," Anna said, as they stepped back into the cool, dark cottage.

"For what, my dear?" Aunt Jacqueline asked, dumping the peas into a colander with a satisfying rattle.

"For the lesson," Anna said. And she meant all of it.

Her aunt smiled, a true, deep smile that reached her eyes. "The first of many. Now, off you go. Your exploration time has officially begun."

Anna didn't need to be told twice. The book of fairies was upstairs, its pages full of whispers. And outside, the real world, which seemed to follow her aunt's strange and wonderful rules, was glowing in the morning sun. She had a feeling the two might be connected.

She tucked the book under her arm and headed down the Wandering Path. It felt different this time. Not just the light, which fell in softer... but the air itself seemed thicker, sweeter. New flowers she hadn't noticed yesterday dotted the mossy verges: tiny bell-shaped blooms of periwinkle blue and clusters of star-like white flowers that glowed faintly in the shade. Maybe it's just my imagination, she thought, but the path itself seemed to hum under her feet, a vibration so soft she felt it more than heard it.

She opened the book as she walked, her eyes scanning the elegant, spidery handwriting. It didn't look printed, each page was penned in dark brown ink, with delicate sketches in the margins, a fern frond, a moth's wing, a circle of mushrooms. It wasn't just stories, it felt like a ledger. One passage was titled "On Fairy Rings & Temporal Anomalies." Underneath a beautiful ink sketch of a mushroom circle was a stark warning in bold letters: "Do Not Enter, Lest You Be Lost to Time."

Anna's heart beat a little faster. She closed the book and walked on, her senses heightened.

And then she saw it.

Just off the path, under the shelter of a great, moss-draped oak, was a perfect circle of pale, ivory-capped mushrooms. They stood like tiny domed houses, their gills delicate and precise, enclosing a circle of emerald moss that looked softer than any carpet. The air above it shimmered faintly, like heat haze on a summer road.

She approached slowly, her breath held. Kneeling at the edge, she peered into the center. The space inside felt different, quieter, older. She remembered the warning, but curiosity tugged at her. What would happen if she stepped inside? Would she see them? Would they see her?

As she leaned closer, a movement caught her eye, not in the circle, but just beyond it, in a patch of clover and wood sorrel. A shimmer, quick and liquid, like sunlight glancing off a dragonfly's wing. But when she turned her head fully, there was nothing. Just leaves and light.

She spent what felt like hours there, sitting cross-legged just outside the ring, the book open in her lap. She watched. She waited. She searched the undergrowth for another glimpse of that elusive shimmer. But the woods kept their secrets, offering only the rustle of leaves and the distant call of a bird.

Eventually, the light began to soften, and Anna knew she should head back. With one last, longing look at the fairy ring, she stood, brushed the moss from her trousers, and carefully marked the spot in her mind: the oak with the split trunk, the foxglove guard, the circle of ivory.

She carried the secret back with her like a treasure, warm and glowing in her chest.

The afternoon light faded from gold to amber as Anna sat beneath the apple tree in the garden, the unopened book now in her lap. The garden seemed to hold its breath with her. Every rustle of leaves, every chirp of a cricket, felt significant, like a coded message she was on the verge of understanding. She stayed there until the shadows grew long and pooled in the hollows, and her aunt's voice called her in for the "evening rounds."

Dinner was a simple soup, its rich broth full of the evening-picked beetroots and carrots, their sweetness deepened by the day's sun. They ate in companionable silence, the weight of Anna's discovery a silent, glowing sphere between them. She wanted to tell her aunt about the mushroom ring, the shimmer, but the words felt too new and fragile, like a soap bubble that might pop if spoken aloud.

After washing the bowls, Aunt Jacqueline didn't light a lamp. Instead, she took two small, handled baskets from a hook. "Come on. Time to gather the night's whispers."

Puzzled, Anna followed her back outside. The world was washed in deep blue and silvery grey. Fireflies had begun their silent, sporadic telegraph in the long grass. Aunt Jacqueline led her not to the vegetable patch, but to a border of flowers Anna had only admired from afar during the day.

"Evening Primrose," her aunt said softly, kneeling beside a plant with tall stems and clusters of pale, closed buds. "She's a shy lady. Only opens for the moon and the moths. Her oil is a powerful healer. But you have to ask politely, and you have to be quiet."

She demonstrated, her hands moving with a slow, reverent precision. She didn't just grab. She cupped a bud gently, her thumb stroking the seam where the petals were tightly furled. She whispered something too low for Anna to hear, a breath, not words. As Anna watched, spellbound, the bud began to tremble. Then, with a silent, graceful unfurling that seemed to take a lifetime, the pale-yellow petals opened to the twilight, releasing a delicate, lemon-sweet scent into the cool air.

"Now she's ready," Jacqueline murmured. With a tiny pair of scissors, she snipped a few of the freshly opened flowers and laid them in her basket. "She'll give us her medicine freely, now that she's been seen."

Anna knelt beside her, her heart pounding. This was no gardening tip. This was a ceremony.

"Your turn," her aunt said, her voice a warm note in the dark. "Choose one. Be gentle. Be present."

Anna's hand shook slightly as she reached out. She selected a plump, closed bud. Mimicking her aunt, she cradled it, feeling the cool, living silk of its surface. She didn't know what to say, so she poured her feelings into her touch: her wonder, her gratitude, the strange awe of the afternoon. Please, she thought. Show me your secret.

She held her breath. For a moment, nothing happened. Then, a faint, answering pulse seemed to travel from the stem into her fingertips. Slowly, magically, the petals began to peel back, unfurling right there in her palm like a secret being confessed.

A gasp caught in Anna's throat. She looked up, her eyes wide, to find her aunt watching her, a profound, knowing smile on her face.

"You see?" Aunt Jacqueline said softly. "It's not about having a green thumb. It's about having a listening heart. You've got one, Anna. I knew it the moment you arrived."

In that moment, under the darkening sky with a night-flower blooming in her hand, Anna felt a trust slot into place, deep and sure. This woman wasn't just quirky. She understood the hidden language of the world. And she was telling Anna she could understand it, too.

They finished gathering in a silence that was full, not empty. Back in the warm, dark kitchen, Aunt Jacqueline laid the evening primroses on a clean cloth. "For a salve," she said. "Good for cuts, for sadness, for dreams that need soothing."

As they climbed the stairs to bed, Anna paused on the landing. "Aunt Jacqueline?" she asked, the question she'd held all day finally finding its courage. "That story you told yesterday... about saving a fairy from a spider's web. When you were a girl."

Her aunt turned, her face half in shadow. The playful twinkle was gone, replaced by a seriousness Anna hadn't seen before. "Yes?"

"Was it... was it just a story?"

Aunt Jacqueline was silent for a long moment, her eyes seeming to look at something far away. Then she reached out and brushed a strand of hair from Anna's forehead, her touch lingering. "The best stories, my dear," she whispered, her voice like the rustle of the primrose leaves, "are the true ones. Now off to bed. Tomorrow is a new day for listening."

Anna lay in the dark for a long time, the scent of primrose clinging to her fingers. She no longer felt like a visitor, or even just a niece. She felt like an apprentice to a beautiful and terrible mystery. And tomorrow, she would listen harder than ever before.

CHAPTER 3: The Wandering Path

Anna woke not to the gentle drift of consciousness, but with a snap, as if her mind had been waiting for the first bird's chirp to throw off the covers. The events of the previous day, the fairy ring, the shimmer, the night-blooming primrose, crashed over her not as a dream, but as a mission. Lying there in the patchwork cocoon of her new room, she felt a solid warmth in her chest. It was trust. Last night, in the dark with a flower blooming in her hand, something had clicked into place. She wasn't just a guest here. She was an apprentice.

She dressed quickly, her movements quiet and purposeful. The little green book lay on her bedside table. She picked it up, feeling the worn cloth cover beneath her fingers. It wasn't her aunt's book anymore. It was hers. Her guide. Her proof that she wasn't imagining things.

She found a pen, a blank notebook for observations, and a small sketchpad with a pencil tucked into its spine, piling them into a simple, sturdy linen bag that smelled faintly of lavender. By the time she padded downstairs, the cottage was already alive with the sizzle and pop of breakfast. The air was rich with the smell of eggs, butter, and something green and fragrant: chives, perhaps, with a hint of the lemon-thyme that grew by the kitchen step.

"Aunt Jacq."
The name felt comfortable sliding off her tongue, like a bite of apple pie. She didn't have to force it.

"You're bright and early," Aunt Jacq said without turning from the stove. She was flipping something golden in a pan. "Planning an expedition?"

Anna froze on the bottom stair, the bag of books suddenly feeling conspicuous. A flush of silly guilt rose in her cheeks. Her aunt had been nothing but kind and open, but the secret of the shimmer felt too new, too fragile to share. It was a treasure she needed to verify alone first.

"Yes," Anna said, her voice a little too bright. "I ... I saw some special flowers out near the woods yesterday. Really unusual ones. I thought I'd go and draw them. I've never seen anything like them."

It wasn't entirely a lie. The mushrooms were unusual.

Aunt Jacq turned, spatula in hand. Her warm, crinkled eyes swept over Anna's eager face, the full linen bag, the determined set of her shoulders. A slow, knowing smile spread across her face, and a glint, that familiar, mysterious glint, sparkled in her eye.

"Well," she said, turning back to the stove, "a scientific expedition requires proper fuel. I've made a special Elf Omelette. I traded some of our rainbow chard with Sue-next-door for her eggs. Her chickens eat wild seeds and listen to violin music, or so she claims. Makes for wonderful eggs."

They sat at the sun-dappled table. The omelette was indeed wonderful, fluffy and golden, studded with finely chopped herbs that tasted of the garden itself. Anna ate quickly, her mind already racing down the path toward the tree line.

Aunt Jacq sipped her tea, watching her with quiet amusement. "Today's a free day," she announced. "No pressing chores. The garden can look after itself for twenty-four hours. So you can go and draw as many ... flowers ... as you like."

She gave Anna a deliberate, soft wink over the rim of her mug.

Anna blushed, the heat blooming in her cheeks. Her aunt hadn't believed the excuse for a second. But she wasn't angry or suspicious. She was permitting it. Encouraging it, even. The wink felt like a key being handed over.

"Thank you," Anna mumbled, her mouth full of the last buttery bite.

"Just be back before the light gets watery," Aunt Jacq said, the familiar gentle warning in her tone. "And remember … listen more than you look."

With the taste of herbs and freedom on her tongue, Anna shouldered her bag and headed out. She didn't meander through the flowerbeds today. She went straight down the main flagstone path, past the apple tree and through the honeysuckle arch, her eyes locked on the green gloom at the bottom of the garden.

The garden gate was a simple, latched thing of weathered wood. Anna paused, her hand resting on the cool, rough timber. This was the boundary. Beyond it lay the Wandering Path. Beyond it were the fairy ring and the shimmer.

She took a deep breath, pushed the gate open, and stepped through.

The air changed instantly: cooler, damper, heavy with the scent of decaying leaves and fertile, hidden earth. The cheerful chorus of garden birds faded, replaced by the solitary call of a wood pigeon and the rustle of unseen creatures in the undergrowth.

The Wandering Path was little more than a suggestion in the grass and moss, dappled with shifting coins of sunlight. But today, with her purpose clear and her senses humming, the path seemed to know where she was headed. The stones underfoot felt warmer, the way clearer, as if the land itself was guiding her toward the split oak and the fairy ring. The faint hum she'd felt yesterday was stronger now: a soft, deep vibration that traveled up through her soles and into her bones.

Heart hammering with a thrilling mix of fear and excitement, Anna followed it. Her eyes were no longer those of a daydreaming girl, but of a hunter. She scanned the ground for the tell-tale ivory circle, peered into the shadows for a flash of impossible colour.

The woods were waiting. And Anna had finally come to listen.

She found the fairy ring without difficulty. In the daylight, it formed a perfect, eerie circle of pale mushrooms: a silent council ground. This was where the shimmer had been.

Anna settled on a mossy hummock nearby, unpacked her book and journals, and waited. She watched. She listened until her ears strained.

But nothing happened.

The morning lengthened. A wood pigeon's rhythmic coo echoed through the canopy. Bees hummed in a patch of clover. The ordinary, beautiful life of the woods carried on, steadfastly ignoring her hopes. The sharp edge of anticipation dulled into stubborn patience, and then, as the sun climbed higher, into a dull ache of disappointment.

Had it all been a trick of the light? A daydream so vivid it felt real?

With a sigh that was almost a groan, she lay back on the moss, staring up at the patchwork of sky and cloud through the leaves. She let her focus soften, just as Aunt Jacq had suggested.

Listen more than you look.

She listened to the wind's sigh, the rustle of leaves, the distant tap of a woodpecker. She watched the clouds drift, a galleon, a sheep, a sleeping giant.

She was on the verge of giving up, of conceding defeat to the rational world, when she saw it.

Not in front of her, but at the very edge of her vision, near the base of a distant, lightning-scarred oak: a rainbow glimmer, quick and clean as a prism catching the sun. Not the darting hover of a dragonfly. This was different. A contained, liquid shimmer, like light skating across a soap bubble.

Her breath caught. She forced herself not to move, not even her eyes. She held the cloud-gaze, her heart thundering in her chest. Slowly, with infinite care, she turned her head a fraction.

There. Again.

Within the shimmer, a form resolved. Then two.

Two small, radiant figures, no taller than her hand, danced in a shaft of sunlight. They chased motes of pollen that glittered like gold dust, their movements a blend of flight and step so graceful they resembled wind-blown petals. Their wings hummed with a soft, musical frequency, and their laughter, sweet and high-pitched, trickled through the air like the chiming of tiny crystal bells. A scent washed over Anna, crisp and wild like frost and honeysuckle. Where their feet touched the air, tiny sparks of light lingered, fading slowly like dying embers.

The sight was too beautiful, too utterly impossible to witness with restraint. The careful observer within her shattered.

With an involuntary gasp of joy, Anna jumped to her feet.

The reaction was instant. The laughter cut off. The shimmering figures froze, turned as one, and with a speed that left afterimages in the air, darted straight into the fissured bark of the old oak and vanished.

"No! Wait!" Anna cried, already running. She stumbled over roots, her bag forgotten, her pulse roaring in her ears. She skidded to a halt at the tree and pressed her hands against the rough bark, peering into every shadow and crevice.

Nothing.

They were gone. The woods felt suddenly silent, empty, mocking.

Tears of frustration stung her eyes. She'd scared them. She'd been too loud, too human, too clumsy. She leaned her forehead against the cool tree, despair washing over her.

Then the habits of a true researcher, honed by years of nature journals and careful inspection, reasserted themselves.

Look. Really look.

She blinked back the tears and examined the tree with meticulous care, running her fingers over the grooves in the bark. At first, it seemed like ordinary oak: rough, cold, real. But then, near the base of the crack, her thumb caught on a ridge that was too smooth, too perfect. The pattern of the bark repeated itself: a clever forgery. She pressed, and the texture gave slightly, like stiff canvas. A concealed flap, woven from lichen and cunning pigment. A painted curtain disguising a deeper opening.

A doorway.

The overlapping split in the trunk was a secret the tree had kept for centuries.

Anna approached, her heart a frantic drum. She placed a hand on either side of the crevice. The bark was warm, unlike the cool forest air, and the hum she'd felt before was stronger here: a subtle vibration traveling up her arms.

She took one last look at the ordinary woods behind her, the world of packed lunches, schoolyards, and quiet worries, then turned sideways, drew in a breath, and edged into the gap.

It was a tight, breathless squeeze. Polished inner wood pressed against her chest and back. For three terrifying heartbeats she was stuck in total darkness, the earthy scent of the tree overwhelming, sap and ancient rain and deep, silent growth.

Then, with a final push, she popped free.

She stumbled forward, `not onto the mossy forest floor beyond the oak, but onto a soft, springy turf of emerald-green grass glowing with its own faint light. The air rushed from her lungs in a stunned exhale.

She was in a forest, but not as she had ever dreamed.

The trees were colossal, their trunks as wide as castle towers, veined with shimmering lichen. Flowers the size of dinner plates pulsed with bioluminescent light. The air itself was thicker, sweeter, charged with an energy that lifted the hair on her arms and tasted of wild apples and lightning. It was beautiful, but beneath the beauty ran a current of wild, untamed power: the feeling of walking through a dream that could turn fierce at any moment.

High above, through a canopy of copper, violet, and deepest jade, two pearl-white moons hung in a twilight-blue sky. And in the distance, dominating the heart of the forest, stood a tree so vast it made the others seem like saplings: its trunk broad and grey as a cliff face, its branches adorned with leaves of silver and gold.

It hummed with a silent, ancient power that Anna felt in her bones.

The awe that held her frozen was sublime: terrifying, beautiful.

A sharp, bell-like giggle, unmistakably from the clearing, cut through her wonder.

The fairies!

For a split second, Anna remembered the warning in the book, Aunt Jacq's voice, the weight of her own curiosity. But the laughter chimed again, tugging at her heart. I have to know. I have to see.

And she ran.

She didn't see the sinuous, scaled shape coiled in the feathery blue bracken beside the path. She didn't hear the warning hiss.

There was only a sudden, searing explosion of pain in her left ankle, as if two red-hot needles had been driven deep into the bone.

A choked cry tore from her throat. She looked down, her vision already blurring.

A creature like a slender, jewelled lizard clung to her sock. Its scales were iridescent, shifting from emerald to oil-slick black in the strange light, and its intelligent eyes, a venomous gleaming yellow, held a spark of unmistakable malice. Its fangs were sunk deep into her skin.

The world tilted. Colours smeared into a sickening vortex. Pain radiated up her leg, a burning cold spreading like spilled ink. The distant giggling sounded as though it came from underwater.

Her legs gave way.

The last thing she saw was the glowing green grass rushing up to meet her.

CHAPTER 4: The Healer's Debt

Anna's consciousness returned in fragments, each one dipped in pain and delirium.

A sensation of floating, cradled by something softer than air. Muffled, chiming voices. "Is it dying?" "She's so big..." "Aunt Laylor will be so cross..."

Then a cooler, clearer voice, like water over stone: "Hush. Carry her gently. To my glade. Quickly."

Blessed coolness on the fire in her ankle. A pungent, green smell that cut through the sickly sweetness of the enchanted air: the scent of crushed herbs, damp earth, and something sharp like lightning. The burning cold of the venom receded, chased away by a deep, throbbing warmth that spread up her leg and through her weary body.

Anna opened her eyes.

A figure was bent over her ankle, hands moving with a fluid, precise grace. Hair the colour of crushed rose quartz, streaked with bold emerald, fell in soft waves around a face lined with age and sharp intelligence. Her wings, large, delicate, and patterned like a lacewing's, were half-unfurled, catching the glade's gentle light. She was the fairy from the painting, but alive, real, and radiating a calm, formidable power.

She was applying a luminous, gold-flecked salve to Anna's ankle with careful, precise fingers.

Memory crashed back: the glorious forest, the searing pain, the jewelled lizard with intelligent, hateful eyes. A jolt of fear went through Anna. She tried to pull her leg back, and her hand clenched instinctively around what she was holding. The book. She'd never let it go.

"You … " Anna's voice was a dry croak. "You … bit me."

The fairy's hands didn't stop their work, but her eyes lifted to meet Anna's. They were stern, but not unkind. "No, child," she said, her voice like the rustle of ancient parchment and flowing water. "I am mending the bite. That was a snappledragon. A foolish, territorial creature with venom for brains. You stumbled into its patch." She finished applying the salve and sat back, her expression hardening as she looked past Anna. "The blame lies with my reckless grandnieces."

Anna followed her gaze. Hovering near a wall of giant ferns, looking thoroughly ashamed, were the two fairy children from the clearing. Their gossamer wings drooped.

"You know you are not to play at The Loose Stitch," the elder fairy said, her voice low with disappointment. "It is not a game. It is a responsibility. A human child, seeing us, crossing over … do you understand the trouble you could have brought down upon us all?"

The blue-haired fairy sniffled. "We're sorry, Aunt Laylor. We didn't think she could really see us. Not properly."

"That is no excuse," the elder fairy, Laylor, sighed, the anger leaving her, replaced by weary concern. "Go. Fetch water from the singing spring. And think about the weight of walls."

The two zipped away, chastened. Laylor turned back to Anna, her expression softening again. "Now, let us see to you properly. The worst is past. The balm draws out the venom and knits the flesh."

Her eyes drifted to the book still clutched in Anna's white-knuckled grip. A flicker of recognition, sharp, sudden, and profound, passed over Laylor's face. Her gaze snapped from the worn cloth cover to Anna's face, searching.

"Where did you get this?" Laylor's voice was barely a whisper.

"My ... my aunt's house," Anna managed. "It was on a shelf."

Laylor reached out, not to take it, but to gently trace the edge of the cover with a fingertip. "This is no common storybook," she murmured, almost to herself. "This is a Hawthorne Folio. The script, the ink ... I know this hand." Her twilight eyes met Anna's, filled with a new, deepening intensity. "Hawthorne. That is your mother's family name, is it not?"

Anna nodded, confused. "My grandmother's maiden name, yes. How did you ... ?"

Laylor's gaze was unwavering. "The woman who wrote this book, Eleanor Hawthorne, was the last human to chart the Glimmer flows with such clarity. She had the Sight, like you. She was a chronicler, a scholar of our world. And she was your kin."

The revelation landed in Anna's chest like a stone. The book wasn't just a curious antique. It was an heirloom. A manual. A legacy.

"You have her eyes," Laylor said, her voice softening once more, but now layered with a new respect. "And Jacqui's eyes."

The name, spoken here with such familiarity, was another shock. "You ... you know my Aunt Jacqueline?"

A profound emotion, a mixture of joy, sadness, and deep gratitude, passed over Laylor's face. "Know her? Jacqui saved my life when I was not much older than those two scamps. A warspider's web, in your world. I was caught, dying. She did not see my magic, but she saw my struggle. She used a stick, gently, so gently, to break the strands. She cupped me in her hands and blew warmth onto my wings until I could fly again." Laylor's voice grew thick. "A debt of life. The oldest and strongest kind. It binds us."

"We watch over her," Laylor continued, her gaze distant. "A little blessing on her crops, a song for her bees. It is a small return. Her garden thrives. Her heart, though worried for her sister, remains kind. It is our way."

"Your sister ... " Anna whispered, the pieces clicking together with a terrible clarity. "My mom. She doesn't believe..."

Laylor's face darkened with a sorrow that was ages old. "Belief is a shield, child. And the lack of it..." She paused, choosing her words with care. "The lack of it can leave a door unlocked. But that is a story for another time, when you are stronger." She leaned forward, her gaze holding Anna's. "Now, a new debt is made. I owe a debt to Jacqui, and you are her blood. You should not be here. This world is not for human children. But you are here, and I will not let harm come to you."

She placed a hand, cool and light as a leaf, on Anna's forehead. "Sleep now. The magic works better with sleep. You are safe here, with me."

The warmth from the balm spread through Anna's whole body, a comfortable, heavy blanket. The terror was gone. The confusion remained, but it was now wrapped in a stunning new truth: magic was real, it was ancient, and it was tied to her family by bonds of bravery, kindness, and ink on a page.

As her eyes fluttered shut, the last thing she saw was Laylor, the fairy with rose-quartz and emerald hair, keeping watch over her, one hand resting near the Hawthorne book: a silent, steadfast guardian in a world of wonders, connecting the past to the present, and Anna to a legacy she was only beginning to understand

CHAPTER 5: The Price of Wonder

Anna slept, but it was not an ordinary sleep. Laylor's touch had drawn her into a deep, dream-filled tide where reality softened at the edges. She dreamed of spidery brown ink forming words on yellowed paper, Nell Hawthorne, 1898, and of towering trees whose leaves were silver constellations. She dreamed of hummingbirds, their wings a prismatic blur, carrying something urgent through a veil of green light.

In the waking world, Laylor did not rest. She withdrew a small, hollowed hawthorn pod from her satchel and breathed into it, her whisper weaving into the still air of the glade. Two hummingbirds, no larger than her thumb, materialized from the dappled light. Their feathers shimmered with captured rainbow, and their eyes held quick, intelligent sparks.

"Find Jacqui," Laylor murmured. "Show her the way. Her heart will know why."

The hummingbirds dipped once in understanding, then shot away, vanishing into the overlapping split of the ancient oak, the Loose Stitch between worlds.

Aunt Jacq was in the garden, her hands buried in the soil of the herb bed, but her mind was far away. A deep, unshakable unease had settled in her chest the moment the afternoon light had turned watery. It was more than worry, it was a pull, a silent scream in a language only her bones understood.

When the hummingbirds appeared, zipping over the honeysuckle arch in a streak of iridescence, she didn't startle. She stood, wiping her hands on her trousers, her heart hammering a single word: Anna.

They danced before her, leading her not to the garden gate, but straight to the Wandering Path. But before she stepped onto it, a flash of color caught her eye, a simple linen bag half-hidden in the ferns just off the flagstones. Anna's bag. The one she'd seen her niece pack that morning with notebooks and pencils.

A cold dread, sharp as a thorn, pierced Jacqui's chest. Anna would never have left it behind. Not willingly. She snatched it up, clutching it to her as if it were a piece of Anna herself.

Then she turned to the Path.

And the Path ... the Path changed. No longer a meandering suggestion, it became a clear, purposeful ribbon through the undergrowth, the moss glowing softly under her feet, the stones warm and aligned. It remembered her. It remembered the debt. It led her without a single twist straight to the great beech tree with the overlapping split.

Without hesitation, bag in hand, she stepped through.

The transition was swift for her, a woman who had always lived with one foot in the unseen. She emerged into the Enchanted Realm, the two hummingbirds now circling her head like living jewels, and followed their lead to Laylor's glade.

When she saw Anna asleep on the velvet moss, pale but whole, the breath left her lungs in a shuddering rush. Then her eyes took in the rest: the glowing mark on Anna's ankle, the old book clutched in her hand, and Laylor, her Laylor, older, wiser, but with the same rose-quartz and emerald hair, keeping watch.

"Jacqui," Laylor said, her voice a blend of relief and sorrow.

Jacqui fell to her knees beside Anna, her hand hovering over her niece's brow. "Is she … "

"She is healed. The venom is gone. But the consequences are just beginning."

They spoke in hushed, urgent tones as the twin moons rose. Laylor explained the snappledragon, the foolish fairies, the debt.

"I owed you, Jacqui," Laylor said, her twilight eyes serious. "A life for a life. Now, because she is your blood and was harmed under my protection, in my realm, the debt extends to her. Debts cascade. They must be honored, or the balance of the Glimmer sickens."

"I didn't save you for a debt, Laylor," Jacqui whispered, her voice thick. "I saved you because it was right."

"I know," Laylor replied, a soft smile touching her lips. "That is why the debt is pure. And why the consequences are now … complicated."

It was then that Anna stirred, the conversation drawing her up from the depths of her magical sleep. Her eyes opened, focusing first on Aunt Jacq's worried face, then on Laylor.

"You're here," Anna rasped.

"I'm here," Jacqui said, squeezing her hand. "We both are."

Anna pushed herself up, the Hawthorne book still in her grip. "Laylor said … the book was my great-grandmother's. That she could see, like me."

Jacqui's eyes met Laylor's over Anna's head. A silent understanding passed between them, a lineage revealed, a legacy awakened.

Before they could say more, the air in the glade thickened. The gentle hum of the forest dimmed, replaced by a profound, watchful silence. A few feet away, the space between two giant ferns shimmered like a heat haze, then tore open with a soft shimmer-rip sound.

From the portal stepped a figure that was decidedly not a fairy.

He was roughly the size of a large badger but stood upright on two legs, clad in a severely cut jacket of grey moss-cloth. His face was furred and shrewd, his eyes the colour of wet slate, holding no nonsense. Intricate miniature medals were pinned to his lapel. In one paw, he held a scroll that glowed with a soft, internal light: the living script of the Great Tree.

"Healer Laylor. Human Jacqueline Hawthorne Davis," he said, his voice a dry, gravelly rasp. "And the human child, Anna. I am Field Agent Tulliver, Bureau of Magic and Mystical Creatures. The Great Tree felt the breach: a human crossing, unauthorized magical intervention. A pulse was sent through the Glimmer network. I am here to enact the law."

Jacqui moved instinctively closer to Anna. "What breach? She was hurt, she was healed!"

"Precisely," Tulliver said, unrolling the scroll. The glowing text shifted and reformed. "A human entered the Enchanted Realm without sanction. She received fairy magic: a healing of significant power. The law, as stored in the Root-Script of the Great Tree, is clear. Knowledge of our world is a contagion. It cannot be allowed to spread unchecked. It must be contained or excised."

He looked directly at Anna. "You have two paths. One: Unmaking. A complex charm will remove all memory of this place, from the moment you saw the juveniles. You return home believing you twisted your ankle in a rabbit hole after a vivid dream."

"No," Anna and Jacqui said simultaneously.

"I thought not," Tulliver said, sounding almost weary. "Option two: Conditional Enchantment. You keep your memory. You may, under strict supervision, return. But you will bear the Ministry's Seal: a Mark of Secrecy, magically enforced. Your healing mark," he pointed a claw at the glowing heart on Anna's ankle, "has already woven a thread of our magic into your essence. It can be adapted. Formalized."

Laylor rose, her wings flaring. "The mark I gave her is one of protection, Tulliver. To warn her. To connect her to the natural Glimmer. Not to shackle her!"

"Your compassion is noted, Healer," Tulliver replied, his tone immutable. "But compassion broke the law today. Now the law must mend the break. The Ministry will decide the Seal's purpose. Magic given must be magic accounted for. That is the first law."

He rolled the scroll shut with a definitive snap. "This is no longer a glade matter. It is a matter for the Grove of Adjudication, at the foot of the Great Tree itself. The local

Elder will hear it, and a ruling will be inscribed into the Root-Script. You will all come. Now."

He turned, gesturing toward a path that now glowed with faint, white mushrooms lighting the way deeper into the forest.

Anna looked from Laylor's defiant face to Aunt Jacq's protective one, then down at the book in her hands: her great-grandmother's legacy. She felt the warm pulse of the mark on her ankle, a thread already tying her to this world.

Tulliver glanced back, his slate-grey eyes resting on her. "Prepare yourself, human child," he said, his gravelly voice echoing in the silent glade. "You are about to learn the price of wonder."

CHAPTER 6: THE WEIGHT OF LAWS

The Grove of Adjudication was not a place one walked to quickly. The Enchanted Forest unfolded around them as they followed a winding path of luminous, white stones. Agent Tulliver led the way, his pace brisk and no-nonsense. Anna walked between Aunt Jacqueline and Laylor, who floated at shoulder height, her wings a soft, humming blur.

The wonders were relentless. They passed a stream where the water flowed upwards over a rock, laughing to itself. They saw trees whose leaves changed colour as they passed, forming intricate, fleeting patterns. But the awe was now tempered with a knot of anxiety in Anna's stomach.

"Laylor," Anna asked quietly, her eyes on the colossal trunk of the Great Tree growing ever larger before them. "Why is it so ... serious? Why can't I just promise not to tell?"

Laylor's expression was grave. "Because promises can be broken, child, even by good hearts. And the cost of a broken promise in our case is not a scolding. It is fire, and iron, and chains, and the end of all this." She gestured to the glowing forest around them. "The laws in the Root-Script were not written in a time of peace. They were carved in the aftermath of the Second Magic War."

Agent Tulliver grunted from ahead, a sound of grim agreement.

"There are ... others," Laylor continued, her voice dropping. "Not all who wield magic are as content as we are to tend our glades and stay hidden. There are those who remember a time when our kinds walked openly among humans, and they hunger for that power again. And there are humans, the wrong kind of humans, who would hunt us for our wings, our magic, our very essence."

Aunt Jacqueline shuddered. "The stories my grandmother told ... she called them 'the greedy ones'."

"Precisely," Laylor said. "The Accords, the laws Tulliver serves, were born from a pact between all peaceful magical beings to vanish, to protect ourselves. To survive. The Great Tree holds that pact. Its roots remember the wars, the pyres, the betrayals. So its laws are absolute. Secrecy is our first and greatest law. Everything else, the ministries, the agents, the enchantments, exists to serve it."

"And the enemy?" Anna pressed, remembering the dark sorrow in Laylor's eyes when she spoke of her mother's disbelief.

Laylor and Tulliver exchanged a glance. It was the agent who spoke, his voice low and precise, each word a stone dropped into the silence.

"The incident with the warspider was not a random predator," Tulliver began, not breaking his stride. "Our archives, cross-referenced with Healer Laylor's testimony after her rescue, confirm it. The creature was a minor Sundered operative, a watcher. Its primary mission was surveillance of the human dwelling adjacent to a known weak point in the Veil: the Loose Stitch. It was searching for a potential 'key,' a human with latent sensitivity."

He glanced back at Jacqueline, his gaze analytical. "You, human, showed not sensitivity, but something equally problematic, interference. By saving a fairy, you revealed a heart aligned with the Glimmering, and you earned its protection. The warspider's secondary protocol was activated: eliminate the interferer. It attempted to place a blight-curse on you."

Laylor's wings gave a pained flutter. "But my gratitude had already woven a thread of protection around her," she whispered, her voice thick with old guilt. "The curse could not take root. It slid off her spirit … and sought the next closest thing. The sister who shared her roof, her blood, her life."

A terrible silence followed, broken only by the soft crunch of their footsteps on the luminous path.

"The 'curse of bad luck' your family endured," Tulliver stated, his voice devoid of pity, "was a sophisticated, long-term Sundered enchantment. Designed not to kill, but to erode. To create a reservoir of misery, frustration, and despair. It was a strategic placement. They were not just punishing an act of kindness. They were preparing a catalyst. A well of negative emotional energy they could one day tap into to rip the Veil wide open. Your mother was not unlucky. She was a battlefield."

The truth of her family's curse settled over Anna like a cloak of lead. It was heavy. Brutal. Deliberate. Her mother's exhaustion, her father's quiet despair, the constant financial strain, none of it was their fault. It was the poison left behind by a monster her aunt had once thwarted. They had been living on cursed ground, their happiness leached away, feeding a future nightmare

"So you see," Laylor said softly, placing a gentle hand on Anna's arm. "The enchantment the Ministry will place upon you … it is not just to bind you. In a way, it is to protect you.

It marks you as under the Ministry's oversight. It makes you... official. A known variable. It offers a sliver of legitimate protection, even from those shadows."

They emerged into a vast, circular clearing at the very base of the Great Tree. The scale was breathtaking. The roots rose like weathered hills, and in their centre was a natural amphitheatre of smooth, polished wood. Seated on a throne of woven roots was an ancient fairy, even older than Laylor, with a beard of silver moss and eyes that held the patient, slow-moving light of centuries.

"Elder Corbin," Agent Tulliver announced, giving a short, sharp bow.

The Elder's gaze swept over them, lingering on Anna and the glowing mark on her ankle. His voice, when it came, was like deep earth shifting.

"The Tree has felt the disturbance. A human child, marked by fairy magic, stands in the Root-Circle." His eyes found Laylor. "Healer. Your debt to the human woman is known to the roots. But debt does not override law. Speak. Why should this human not be returned to her world ... unmade?"

The formal hearing had begun. The fate of Anna's memory, her connection to this world, and the safety of both her families, now rested on the words to be spoken in this ancient, fearful place.

CHAPTER 7: THE QUIET BETWEEN

The morning after the Grove felt like waking up in a different world, even though Anna was in the same patchwork-quilt bed. Sunlight streamed in, ordinary and golden. The birds sang their usual chorus. For a dizzying moment, she wondered if it had all been an incredibly vivid dream.

Then she moved her ankle. A soft, warm tingle emanated from the hawthorn tree sigil, a living tattoo, its roots seeming to delve into her and its branches reaching up her calf. It pulsed in time with her heartbeat, a constant, gentle reminder etched into her very skin. Not a dream.

She pressed her fingers to it and felt ... a hum. Not just in her skin, but deeper, as if the mark was a taproot connecting her to the slow, patient heartbeat of the earth itself.

Downstairs, the smell of toast and Aunt Jacq's quiet humming floated up. It was the same scene as her first morning, yet everything was different.

They ate breakfast in a comfortable, heavy silence. The weight of the unspeakable sat between them on the wooden table, alongside the butter and jam. As Jacq spread blackberry jam, a bee, dusty with pollen, buzzed in through the open window, circled her head once, and landed briefly on the rim of her cup before flying out. She didn't flinch. She smiled.

"Morning report," she murmured to Anna, and the tension broke a little.

Finally, Jacq spoke, her voice careful. "Does it ... bother you? The mark?"

Anna shook her head. "It feels warm. Like a cat sleeping on my ankle. Connected." She paused. "Does yours?"

Jacqui placed a hand over her heart, where the vine-like tracery of her own ward-mark lay hidden. "Like a small, living locket. Holding a secret." She gave a wry smile. "We're quite a pair, aren't we?"

They cleared the plates, and without discussing it, they both drifted to the back door. The garden awaited, their familiar, beautiful sanctuary. But now, they looked at it with new eyes.

They spent the day in the garden, not working, but being. Anna sat and sketched, not trying to capture fairy shapes, but the incredible, geometric perfection of a bean flower's spiral. Jacqui weeded, her touch even more reverent than before. When she brushed a rosemary bush, it released its scent in a grateful cloud.

"She said they helped it grow," Anna whispered, running a hand over the velvety leaf of a lamb's ear. "Laylor and the others."

"I always thought I just had good soil," Jacqui murmured, kneeling beside a row of impossibly plump strawberries. "And a lot of luck." She pointed to a pea tendril, coiled in a perfect Fibonacci spiral. "Look at that. That's not just growth. That's … a signature."

After a simple lunch, Anna felt a familiar, gentle tug on her senses, not from the garden, but from the Seal on her ankle. It pulsed warmly, a soft, inviting hum that seemed to pull toward the Wandering Path.

"It's calling you, isn't it?" Jacqui said, wiping her hands on a towel. She smiled. "Go. The Path will keep you safe. Just be back before the light changes."

Anna didn't hesitate. She stepped through the garden gate, and this time, the Wandering Path greeted her like an old friend. The stones glowed faintly under her feet, and the air tasted of rain and green growth. It led her unerringly to the Loose Stitch, and with a deep breath, she slipped through the tree.

She emerged not into the vast, intimidating forest of her first visit, but into a small, sun-dappled glade she hadn't seen before. It was clearly a place of gathering. Soft mossy tufts served as seats, and toadstools of various sizes formed tables. A tiny, crystal-clear stream giggled through one side, and the air smelled of honey, crushed mint, and something sweetly spicy: like cinnamon and starlight.

And it was full of life.

Three young fairies (not the two from before, but others) were practicing aerial loops near a willow branch. A stout, badger-like creature in a tiny apron was stirring a steaming pot over a miniature fire of glowing embers. A tree-spirit child with bark-skin and hair of hanging moss was carefully arranging pebbles in a spiral pattern on the ground.

All activity stopped when Anna stepped into the glade.

For a moment, there was only silence. Then, one of the fairies, a boy with dragonfly wings and hair like spun copper, zipped forward, hovering at eye level.

"You're her," he said, his voice a bright chime. "The Hawthorne Heir. The one the Tree spoke to."

Before Anna could respond, the other two fairies joined him, their eyes wide with curiosity, not fear.

"Is it true you have the Glimmer-Words?" a girl with moth-wing patterns asked.

"Can you show us?" the third added, her voice like wind through reeds.

Anna shook her head gently. "I ... I don't know how to open it yet. And I think it's supposed to stay in the Grove."

The badger-like creature, a young Stout-folk, waddled over, holding a tiny clay cup. "Here," she said in a gruff, but not unkind, voice. "Sunbrew. It'll help the newness wear off."

Anna accepted the cup. The drink was warm and tasted of chamomile and sunlight. She took a sip, and a sense of calm spread through her.

"Thank you."

"Name's Marn," the Stout-folk said. "My granddam works in the Root-Script archives. She says your great-grandmother's book is cited in three treatises on Veil integrity." She said it with the gravity of a scholar citing sacred texts.

The tree-spirit child approached shyly, holding out a perfectly round, smooth stone that glowed with a soft blue light. "For you," it rustled. "A remembering-stone. It holds the memory of this glade. So you know you have a place here."

Anna took the stone, and warmth spread from it up her arm. She felt a flash of the glade's peace: the sound of the stream, the smell of the air, the feeling of safety. Her throat tightened.

"I don't know what to say."

"You don't have to say anything," the copper-haired fairy said, landing lightly on her shoulder. His wings tickled her cheek. "You just have to be. That's what Laylor says. 'The Glimmering knows its own.'"

They spent the next hour in easy, simple companionship. Anna learned their names: Copper, Willow, and Luna for the fairies. The tree-spirit was Sapling. They showed her how to weave blades of glow-grass into a bracelet that pulsed softly on her wrist. Marn explained how the embers of their fire were made from compressed sunlight, harvested at dawn.

Anna, in turn, told them about her world, about cars and schools and city parks. They listened, fascinated, asking questions like "What's a television?" and "Do your trees sing?"

For the first time, Anna didn't feel like an intruder or a chosen one. She felt like ... a friend. The Glimmering wasn't just magic. It was community. It was laughter like wind chimes, shared sunbrew, and the offering of a remembering-stone.

When the light in the glade began to shift toward amber, Anna knew it was time to go. She stood, the glow-grass bracelet shimmering on her wrist.

"Thank you," she said, and she meant it with her whole heart.

"Come back," Sapling rustled.

"We'll teach you to speak to stones," Copper chimed.

Anna nodded, her smile genuine. "I will."

The Wandering Path led her home, and as she stepped back into the cottage garden, she felt different. The Glimmering wasn't just out there anymore. It was inside her. It was in the warm stone in her pocket, the bracelet on her wrist, and the memory of new friends who saw her not as a human, but as Anna.

As dusk painted the sky in watercolour hues of peach and lavender, they sat on the stone bench, watching the fireflies awaken.

"Are you scared?" Anna asked, the question she'd been holding all day finally slipping out.

"Terrified," Jacqui admitted, putting an arm around her. "For you. What the book means. What they'll ask of you someday." She squeezed Anna's shoulder. "But also… a little thrilled. To know it's all real. To have her back in my life, even like this. And that book … " Her voice dropped, filled with awe. "The Locked Chapter. That's not just a story anymore, Anna. It's yours."

"But I don't know what it says," Anna said quietly.

"Maybe you're not meant to yet," Jacqui replied. "Maybe it's enough that it chose you."

That night, as Anna lay in bed reading her great-grandmother's book (its pages now felt like letters from a relative she'd never met), a soft glow filled her window. Not moonlight. A pearlescent, pink-and-green shimmer, like sunlight through a stained-glass leaf.

She sat up. Floating outside her window was Laylor, no larger than a sparrow, her wings a soft blur of gossamer and hawthorn-leaf green. She gestured gently toward the garden.

Anna slipped downstairs, meeting Jacqui who was already at the back door, drawn by the same silent call.

Laylor waited for them in the moonlit herb garden, perched on the rosemary bush. She looked smaller here, less the imposing healer, more the secret friend, but her eyes held a new, solemn depth.

"I came to see the garden by moonlight," she said, her voice a melodic whisper. "And to see you both, on the quiet side of the Veil."

"It's all because of you, isn't it?" Jacqui asked, her voice full of emotion. "The garden. The luck. The beauty."

Laylor nodded. "A whisper to the seeds. A song to the worms. A little dust of encouragement on the blossoms. It is the least of repayments." She turned her twilight gaze to Anna. "But we must speak of the Glimmer-Words."

Anna's heart thumped. "Can you read them?"

A shadow of something like reverence passed over Laylor's face. "No. Nor can the Elders. Not truly. The script ... shifts. It is alive. It responds to the reader. When I look upon it, I see beautiful, swirling light, healing patterns from the dawn of magic. When Elder Corbin looks, he sees the unbreakable laws of the Accord. Tulliver sees wards and shields." She floated closer. "The book shows you what you are ready to see. And it has waited a very long time for a Hawthorne with the Sight to stand before it."

"What will I see?" Anna whispered.

"That," Laylor said softly, "is between you and the Tree. But know this: the power in that book is not for casting spells. It is for understanding magic. For hearing its first language. Your training will not be about learning tricks. It will be about learning to listen: to the Glimmer in the soil, in the air, in your own blood. The book will guide you, when you are ready."

She reached out a tiny hand, and a single, glowing mote of light, like a captured firefly, floated from her palm. It split in two, drifting to rest briefly on Anna's and then Jacqui's foreheads, a sensation like a dewdrop kiss that left a tiny, shimmering star that faded after a few seconds.

"A blessing for the road ahead," Laylor whispered. "For both my wards. The quiet between storms is a gift. Cherish it." She winked at Jacqui, a flash of the young fairy the girl had saved. "Goodnight, my friends."

With a soft hum, she was gone, dissolving into the moonlight.

Anna and Jacqui stood in the silent garden, the blessing a cool, comforting spot on their skin. The fear was still there, but it was now wrapped in something stronger: a sense of legacy, of mystery, of a story they were now woven into, waiting for the next page to turn.

CHAPTER 8: THE WAITING

The days after the Grove did not settle into quiet. They thrummed with a new, urgent purpose. The cottage remained a sanctuary of warm bread and lavender, but Anna's true work now began at dawn, on the other side of the Veil.

Her instructor was Elara, a Listener Priestess. She was older than Laylor, her hair the colour of weathered birch, her presence so still she seemed part of the glade itself. Her eyes, pale as morning mist, held neither judgment nor warmth: only profound, patient attention.

"You are a Warden-Apprentice," Elara said on the first morning, her voice the soft scrape of bark on stone. She gestured to the new book Anna carried, the one given by the Great Tree. It was small, bound in what felt like living wood, and sealed with a clasp of intertwined roots. "Your first duty is not to act, but to understand. And your first lesson lies here, in what you cannot yet read."

The book was titled in root-script that shimmered only when Anna focused her will: "On the Unseen Architecture: A Warden's Primer." But the final chapter, the most crucial one, was locked. The clasp would not open.

"The Great Tree does not give keys," Elara said, placing a cool hand over Anna's where it rested on the cover. "It gives paths. The Locked Chapter is written in the language of the Glimmer itself. To read it, you must first learn the language of its roots and rings. You must learn to listen"

Elara began with silence.

Mornings were spent in a sacred grove where the air hummed with invisible energy. With her palm on a warm root of the Great Tree and the locked book on her lap, Anna learned to still her mind. It was harder than it sounded. Her thoughts were noisy things, worries about her parents, excitement about fairies, the strange new weight of the seal on her ankle.

"Listen past your own breath," Elara would murmur. "Listen to the breath of the place."

Slowly, Anna began to hear it. Not with her ears, but through the warm pulse in her ankle. It was a tapestry of sensation, the bright chattering energy where sun struck moss, the deep, slow sigh from the heart of an ancient oak, the quick, silver thrill of a hidden stream. The Glimmer had a texture, a temperature, a mood.

"Today it is content," Anna reported one morning, her eyes closed.

"And how do you know?" Elara asked.

"It's ... humming. In a major key. And the threads feel warm and loose, not tight."

A pause. "Good," Elara said, and the word felt like a prize.

Afternoons were for basic exercises. Elara taught her to extend her awareness, like casting a delicate net, to feel for disturbances. Anna practiced on a wilting fern (its energy thin and frayed), on a patch of poisoned earth Laylor had set aside for training (a sickly, greasy cold), and on the happy, bustling glade where Copper and his friends played (a sparkling, chaotic warmth).

She was learning a new sense, and it was exhausting. But the locked book on her desk was a constant, tantalising promise. Sometimes, in deep meditation, the root-clasp would grow warm. Once, a single glyph on the cover shimmered with a light that seemed to say patience.

One evening, as a soft dusk settled, Anna sat in the cottage garden, attempting to map the gentle currents of home. Her Primer lay beside her, its clasp as stubborn as ever.

The interruption, when it came, was not gentle.

A shadow fell across her notebook. She looked up.

Field Agent Tulliver stood at the garden gate, his grey cloak damp with mist from the Glimmer Realm. He wore practical travel gear, his expression granite, his slate-coloured eyes grimly focused.

"Warden-Apprentice," he rasped. "Your guardian. Now."

A moment later, they faced him at the kitchen table. He placed an ironbark scroll-case stamped with the Bureau's seal on the wood with a definitive thunk.

"The quiet is over," he stated. "The Sundered network is activated. Your parents' home in London is the primary tactical locus for their next breach attempt."

He unrolled the scroll, translating the dense root-script with brutal efficiency. "Operation Catalyst. They will use the residual, curse-born misery around your parents as a link to channel Sundered energy. Their objective: to shatter the Veil at a major London convergence point."

He looked directly at Anna. "The allotment was a test. This is the detonation."

He tapped the scroll. "Priority Directive. Task Force Root & Thorn is formally activated and deployed. Embed within the Davis household. Your mission: fortify the location, intercept the operatives, and contain any breach. At all costs."

His gaze swept over them both. "This is interdiction. Urban terrain. Civilian population. You will learn in real time."

He rolled the scroll up. "We depart in one hour. Essentials only. Laylor rendezvous at the transition point. Prepare."

He turned and left, the scroll-case a tangible weight of impending war on the table.

Anna looked at Jacqueline. Her aunt's eyes held no panic, only fierce resolve. Anna's own fear was a fluttering thing, but beneath it was the new, steady hum of her seal and the silent weight of the locked book.

The waiting was over. The war had not come to her doorstep. They were being sent directly into its heart.

CHAPTER 9: The Moss-Stone Briefing

Dawn at the eastern stream was a world of silver mist and dripping ferns. The Moss-Stone, an ancient slab half-submerged in the bank, was covered in velvet moss that glowed with its own soft, internal light. Anna stood beside Jacqueline, the dawn chill sharp on her skin, but inside she felt a steady, focused warmth. The frantic confusion of the girl who had first stumbled through the Loose Stitch was gone. In its place was a cold, clear understanding, her family had been a target long before she knew magic existed. That knowledge settled in her bones, not as a fear, but as a purpose.

He came without sound.

One moment, the clearing was empty. The next, Agent Tulliver stood upon the Moss-Stone, backlit by the pearly dawn. He wore practical gear of muted forest hues and his long grey coat. His sharp eyes swept over them, pausing on Anna. She met his gaze steadily, her shoulders squared. He gave a minute, almost imperceptible nod, not of greeting, but of assessment. He saw the change.

"Ward. Guardian," he said, his voice the dry rasp of autumn leaves. "Time is a fraying thread. Questions will be answered en route. Our objective, embed you, back into the target environment, your familial dwelling. We identify and neutralize the hostile agent before it enacts Phase Two."

He hopped down, landing with a predator's lightness. "Embedding requires a credible change. The enemy's curse created strain. We reverse it." He said the next words with palpable distaste. "'Operation Gentle Bloom.' Subtle perception-enhancements have been applied to your parents' work, textiles and produce. Their 'luck' has turned. You return to a home of relief. This is our cover."

Anna processed this not with wonder, but with tactical appreciation. It was a clean, clever solution. Magic wasn't just about shimmer and flight, it was about psychology, about mending the very cracks the enemy had exploited. She understood that now.

"And you?" Anna asked, her voice calm. "How do you come with us?"

A flicker of profound annoyance passed over Tulliver's face. He gestured, and a small, lumpy shape floated into view from behind the stone. A stuffed toy badger, with crooked button eyes and worn brown plush.

"This," he said, the words seeming to pain him, "is a Glamour of Inanimacy. To all human senses, I am this ... object. To you, and to any with the Sight, I am myself. You will carry me as a comfort from your aunt's home. You will not address me in the presence of humans. You will listen. Constantly."

Jacqueline stepped forward. "And my role?"

Tulliver's gaze shifted. "You are the emotional conduit and secondary observer. Your cover is a family visit. Your true purpose is to provide stability, run interference, and use your own sensitivity to monitor the environment. You are the guardian. I am the weapon."

He turned, scooped up the badger, and with a complex twist of his free hand, stepped into it. The air shimmered. Where the formidable agent had stood, only the stuffed toy remained, dropping to the moss with a soft plop.

Then one glass-bead eye winked.

"The sprite has returned with our acknowledgement," Tulliver's voice came from the toy, compressed and irritable. "We depart for the human transit point immediately. The train to London leaves in two hours. Keep up."

The journey was a study in controlled tension. On the train, tucked into a quiet compartment, Tulliver's whispered briefing continued. Anna listened, not with the wide-eyed overwhelm of before, but with the focused attention of a soldier. She learned the hostile agent was a Shaper, specializing in emotional resonance.

"The curse was the priming of the pump," Tulliver murmured. "The Shaper will now attempt to release the pressure in a visible, explosive manner. A manifestation. Our job is to find its workshop and dismantle the mechanism."

As the green countryside gave way to London's outskirts, Anna felt the shift viscerally. The air grew thin and sharp. Closing her eyes, she let her Warden's Sight drift open. The dense, harmonious chorus of the Glimmer Realm was gone, replaced by a roaring static of human emotion and the dull, grey ache of concrete suppressing the land's natural pulse. And there, like a throbbing wound, was the familiar, sickly signal from the allotment. Her mark gave a low, sympathetic throb of warning.

Jacqueline squeezed her hand. "It's still there. The Glimmer. It's just ... drowning."
"It's also sick," Anna replied softly, her eyes still closed as she mapped the psychic pollution. "And it's scared."

They arrived at the Davis household in a drizzle of grey rain. The terraced house looked smaller, but different. To Anna's Sight, a gentle, golden haze, the 'Gentle Bloom,' cloaked the brickwork, and the lingering, greasy stain of the old curse was being actively dissolved by it. It was a battlefield being cleansed.

When Emily Davis opened the door, the change was breathtaking. The weariness was gone, her smile unforced. She crushed Anna in a hug. But as Anna hugged her back, she wasn't just feeling relief. She was assessing. She felt the light, healthy buzz of the perception enchantment around her mother, and the faint, almost-healed scar beneath it where the blight-curse had once festered.

"You're here! Oh, things have been so good!" Emily gushed, pulling Jacqueline in next.

Jack appeared behind her, his quiet presence now radiating a solid pride. He ruffled Anna's hair. "Welcome home, love. Proper home, now."

Anna smiled, a real smile, but it was layered. She was happy to see them joyful. But she also saw them now as assets under protection, civilians in a war they couldn't perceive. Her love was fiercer, more protective because of it.

The house felt lighter, the air didn't sag. But to Anna, it was also a new kind of operational zone. Her old room felt like a safe house. She placed the stuffed badger on her pillow, where it looked absurdly out of place: a piece of otherworldly artillery in a room of childhood memories.

That night, after a happy, chatty dinner that Anna navigated with a newfound, observant calm, she lay in the dark. Car headlights swept across the ceiling. A distant siren wailed.

From the pillow came the faintest whisper. "Observation begins at dawn, Warden-Apprentice. Sleep. You will need it."

Anna didn't just hear the order. She acknowledged it. She was no longer waiting for the world to happen to her. She was waiting for the hunt to begin.

The waiting was over. The embedding was complete. The hunt, in the heart of her own home, was about to begin.

CHAPTER 10: The First Pulse

Breakfast was a quiet, sunny affair. Anna pushed scrambled eggs around her plate, her senses tuned not to the taste, but to the gentle, golden hum of the 'Gentle Bloom' enchantment that clung to the butter and the herbs from her father's allotment. It was a peaceful feeling, like a warm blanket over the house.

Then a shadow passed over the window.

A large, jet-black crow landed on the fencepost at the end of the small garden. It didn't peck. It didn't caw. It settled into an unnatural stillness, swivelling its head to fix one gleaming, intelligent eye on the house.

"Oh, him again," Emily said, following Anna's gaze. "He's a regular. Never seems to want anything. Just ... watches."

Jack chuckled. "Maybe he's a critic of my roses."

Aunt Jacqueline put down her tea with a soft clink. Her eyes met Anna's across the table. A silent alarm passed between them.

From the floor where he'd been propped against a chair leg, a low, urgent growl emanated: a sound only they could hear.

"Upstairs. Now. All of you. Casual-like."

Anna forced a smile, her heart beginning a steady, tactical drumbeat against her ribs. "I'm full. Can I be excused? I want to finish my book."

"Of course, love," Emily said, her attention already drifting back to the newspaper.

Jacqueline stood, gathering plates with a calm so deliberate it felt like a performance. "I'll help you clear, Em. Let's give the menfolk the washing up for once."

A minute later, Anna and Jacqueline were in Anna's room, the door shut. Anna grabbed the stuffed badger from her bed and held it up to the window, peeking through a narrow gap in the curtains.

The crow was still there, a statue of polished darkness.

"Describe it," Tulliver's voice was a tense whisper from the toy. "Not with your eyes. With your Sight."

Anna closed her eyes, letting the warm pulse in her ankle expand into a listening shell. She pushed past the comforting gold of the 'Gentle Bloom,' past the bright, loving buzz of her family's presence. She sought the discord.

It wasn't just a hole. It was active.

"It's ... probing," she whispered, struggling to articulate the sensation. "A cold, thin feeling, like an icy finger. It's brushing over the house, It touched the happy feeling we made and recoiled. It's confused. Now it's pressing harder, focusing, It's found something sad,In the front hallway."

"Precision reconnaissance construct," Tulliver grunted, a sound of grim professional respect. "A Messenger. It's tasting the mood of the place. Checking if the misery it expects is still here. Our happiness is a surprise. It's investigating the surprise. Which means the thing that makes the sadness is inside this house. Find it. Before the Messenger finishes its taste-test and flies home. If it does, the next visitor will be a detonation team."

The cozy bedroom became a glass box under a lidless eye. The enemy wasn't at the door. Its lens was on the fence. And its microphone was in their walls.

"We must be systematic," Tulliver instructed as they crept downstairs. "Ward, lead, follow the coldest thread. Healer, guard the rear. Watch the windows."

Anna moved into the hallway, her breathing shallow. She pushed aside the warm domestic feelings, the citrus-scent of cleaning spray, the faint, happy buzz from the kitchen. She sought the discord, the empty, sucking cold the probe was homing in on.

It pulsed, a weak, frozen heartbeat. Not from the cupboard. Not from under the stairs.

Her gaze travelled up the worn hat-and-coat rack by the front door. Amongst the scarves and caps hung a small, carved wooden bird, darkened with age and dust.

"There," she breathed, pointing.

Jacqueline sucked in a sharp breath. "That old thing? It's been there forever. A charity shop find."

"Precisely," Tulliver murmured. "Deep-cover surveillance. A feeling-snare. The curse gave it a purpose. Your newfound peace has made it scream." His glass eyes seemed to analyze the carving. "A trap for gloom. For years, it drank your family's worry. Now your joy is poison to it. It's shaking itself apart, and that shaking is what the crow feels."

"How do we stop it?" Anna whispered, her eyes darting to the front window, half-expecting the crow to be perched on the sill.

"We must replace the feeling. Give it what it expects. Make it taste the old, cursed sorrow again, but we will control the recipe." He turned his head towards Anna. "This is applied theory. Project a memory of the misery over the device. I will guide you. One pulse of your true fear, and it will shatter, sending a final, catastrophic scream."

Anna's mouth was dry. "How?"

"You lived it. Your mark remembers what this house felt like. Find that memory. The heavy silence. The sour smell of worry. Channel that old feeling through your mark and into the snare. Not to curse it, but to disguise it."

With Jacqueline's body blocking the view from the front window, Anna approached the coat rack. She raised a trembling hand, hovering an inch from the carved bird. A biting cold radiated from it.

"Now," Tulliver said, his voice a steadying anchor in her mind. "Find the memory. The grey feeling."

Anna closed her eyes. She didn't just remember, she reconstructed. The way her mother's smiles never reached her eyes. The specific sigh her father made when he thought no one was listening. The leaden weight in the air every month when the bills arrived. She gathered that heavy, grey gloom, not as her own emotion, but as a ghost of the past, and willed it down through her body, into the warm, rooted mark on her ankle.

The mark responded. Instead of its usual green-gold warmth, it thrummed with a thin, precise ache: a perfect echo of the blight-curse's sorrow. She directed it up her arm, out through her fingertips.

A faint, illusory shadow washed over the carved bird. The sucking cold in Anna's senses muted, replaced by a dull, familiar throb of simulated sadness. The bird gave an almost imperceptible shudder and fell still, its surface appearing even dustier, more forgotten.

"Hold it," Tulliver whispered. "Steady. You are ghosting a memory. Making it taste the past."

Sweat beaded on Anna's temples. The effort was immense, a delicate, agonizing balance of power and precision. She was a forger, painting a masterpiece of misery with a brush of pure will.

Finally, Tulliver grunted. "It is done. The snare tastes stable despair. The anomaly is clearing." He paused, listening to a silence only he could hear. "The probe is withdrawing. Slowly, release the thread."

Anna let the grey feeling fade, pulling her energy back into herself with a gasp. She stumbled back, a sharp headache blooming behind her eyes. Jacqueline caught her, an arm tight around her shoulders.

They watched the carved bird. It hung, inert, just a piece of junk once more.

From the garden, a rustle of wings. They peeked through the hall window. The crow on the fencepost tilted its head once, its gleaming eye now holding only avian blankness. With a dismissive caw, it launched into the air and flew away, its mission concluded with a false report.

The immediate threat had passed. They had successfully lied to the enemy's tongue.

Anna slumped against her aunt, exhausted, but a fierce, bright pride burning in her chest. She hadn't just sensed magic. She had weaponized memory.

Tulliver's voice broke the silence, gruff but with a faint note of something that might have been approval. "Lesson one: counter-intelligence. Passed."

The pride in Anna's chest curdled, replaced by a cold, sinking realization. She hadn't just saved them. She had confirmed the enemy's weapon was armed.

As if reading her thoughts, Tulliver's voice cut through the quiet, colder than the Messenger's gaze. "Do not mistake survival for victory, Warden-Apprentice. We have fed the enemy the lie it wanted to taste. It now believes its catalyst, this house, your family's misery, is ripe and potent. It will not send another taster. It will proceed to ignite it. We have not stopped the attack. We have set the timer."

Anna looked from the harmless-looking carved bird to the cheerful kitchen, where her parents' muffled laughter echoed. The warm pulse in her ankle now felt less like a comfort and more like the steady, ominous ticking of a countdown she had just accelerated.

The battle in the house was won. The war for the city had just entered its most dangerous phase.

CHAPTER 11: The Allotment Ambush

The community allotment was a patchwork quilt of green in a sea of grey brick. To Anna, walking the gravel path with her aunt and her ominously silent bag, it felt like a ghost. The vibrant, living Glimmer she now associated with growth was thin here, strained. It pooled in Jack's thriving plot, but even that felt ... contained, as if held behind glass.

And at the centre of his plot stood the scarecrow.

It was a ramshackle thing, Jack's old coat on crossed poles, a sack for a head. But to Anna's senses, it was a stillness. A perfect, circular void where the gentle hum of life should be.

"Report," Tulliver's voice grumbled from the bag, a private command.

"It's not ... doing anything," Anna whispered, confusion warring with dread. "It's just a hole. A cold, silent hole in the middle of everything."

"That is the problem," Tulliver replied. "A Sundered construct is never inert. It is either active, or it is a shell. Healer, keep your eyes on it. Ward, sweep the perimeter. Look for other wrong feelings. Map the sickness."

Anna nodded, turning her focus outward. She let her Warden's Sight expand, filtering the noise. The allotment's feeling was a sad, thin whisper. It should have hummed with pride and growing things, but instead it felt frayed and anxious, buzzing with the gardeners' hidden worries. Beneath that, the deep, slow pulse of the land itself felt weak and sick, like it was being sucked dry.

Then, a jab. Sharp, urgent, and wrong. From the far end of the allotment, near a rotting compost bin, a pulse of unmistakable Sundered energy flared, a spike of sickly green in her mind's eye. It was stronger than the scarecrow's emptiness. It felt active, a hungry pump attached to a vein.

"Contact," she hissed. "Secondary source. By the compost. It's... buzzing. Like it's feeding on something."

Tulliver was silent for a beat. "A relay. Or a power source syphoning the land's deep strength. It must be mapped. Healer, maintain visual on the primary. Ward, you will approach the secondary with me. Do not lose sight of your aunt."

It felt like a mistake even as they did it. The distance between the scarecrow and the compost heap was only fifty yards, but it felt like a canyon. Anna kept looking back, seeing Jacqueline's steady figure by the fence, her hand resting on a post, watching the scarecrow.

Then, when Anna was halfway, the world bent.

It was silent. One moment, the path was clear. The next, the air between the plots shimmered, like heat haze off tarmac, but cold. Through the distortion, Jacqueline's figure wavered, fractured, and then vanished entirely.

"Visual contact lost!" Tulliver's snarl was sharp with alarm. "A Shaper's Weave, a 'Weave of Isolation'! It's twisting the local paths to create a maze! The scarecrow is the generator! Back to the Healer, now!"

Anna spun to run back, but the path was gone. The neat rectangular plots twisted into a confusing labyrinth of towering bean poles and shivering kale. A faint, grey fog, smelling of damp concrete and ozone, coiled up from the ground.

"Aunt Jacq!" Anna shouted, her voice swallowed by the dead air.

No answer.

Then, the fog directly in front of her parted, not clearing, but forming a perfect, still circle. And in that circle, the allotment died.

The soil turned ashen. The plants withered to grey husks. And from the crumbling compost heap, the rusted water tank, the very shadows of the fence, something drew itself together.

Krawl did not step forward. It precipitated. A figure of packed soot and crumbling mortar, strung with tendons of rusty wire, draped in tattered, oil-slick feathers that were not feathers but shards of corrupted shadow. Its face was a suggestion of features in slag and cracked tile, and in the sockets, two pinpricks of venomous green light fixed on Anna.

"Little root." The voice was the groan of a settling building, the skitter of rats in plaster. "All alone in the false garden. Where is your soldier? Where is your earth-witch? Just you. And the rot."

Anna's breath froze in her chest. She tried to reach for her Glimmer, to push back with a memory of grey, with anything. But the dead circle was a null-field. The warm hum in her ankle guttered, choked. She was cut off from the living world. The power she'd so recently discovered was gone, leaving only the cold sweat of mortal fear.

Krawl took a step, a grinding, gritty sound. It raised a hand that was more like a cluster of rusted rebar. "The sapling will be plucked before it learns to stand."

Outside the distortion field, Jacqueline's world had gone silent. One second Anna was there, the next, a wall of shimmering, sickly air.

"Anna!" Her shout was raw. She ran forward, but the air pushed back, elastic and greasy.

Panic, cold and pure, shot through her. Then, a searing pain bloomed over her heart: the vine-like mark Laylor had given her. It wasn't a warning. It was a scream in the silent language of the bond. Anna's terror.

Magic. Fairies. Seals. It all vanished from her mind. There was only one truth: her niece was in mortal danger, and the enemy was the thing twisting brother-in-law's garden.

She didn't look at the shimmering field. She looked at the source. The scarecrow. The void. The thing poisoning this place.

Jacqueline dropped to her knees in Jack's lovingly tended soil. She didn't chant spells. She poured her will, her love, her years of talking to green things into the earth. She grabbed two fistfuls of rich, dark loam.

"NO!" she roared, her voice not loud, but immensely present. "This is not your place! This is Jack's place! This is where things grow! You do not get to take it! YOU DO NOT GET TO TAKE HER!"

She slammed her hands, full of living soil, onto the base of the scarecrow's pole.

A shockwave, silent and invisible to human eyes, erupted. Not of Glimmer, but of absolute, defiant belonging. The scarecrow didn't break. It shattered. The old coat burst into dust and rags. The sack-head disintegrated. The poles splintered into dry, dead sticks.

The shimmering field around Anna flickered and tore like rotten silk.

Inside the dead circle, Krawl's claws were inches from Anna's face when it jerked back, its form rippling as if struck by a physical blow. The green lights of its eyes flared with shock and pain. The null-field sputtered. The connection to her ankle, to the living world, rushed back into Anna with a dizzying, painful surge.

"ANNA! HERE!" Jacqueline's voice, real and close, cut through the dying fog.

Tulliver's command was a bark of pure survival instinct.

"RUN! TO THE COTTAGE! NOW! DO NOT LOOK BACK!"

Anna didn't need telling twice. She turned and ran, her feet slipping on the gravel, her lungs burning. She crashed through the last tatters of the distortion field and saw Jacqueline, still kneeling in the soil, her hands black with earth, her face streaked with tears and fury.

No words. Jacqueline grabbed her arm, and they ran, leaving the allotment behind. In the echoing silence of their flight, they heard one last sound: a grinding, furious shriek that seemed to come from the stones and the rust itself.

They had not won. They had escaped. And they were now being hunted in earnest.

The retreat to the Enchanted Realm was no longer an option. It was the only path left.

CHAPTER 12: The Home Front

The plan formed in desperate, urgent breaths.

"You can't take the train," Jack said, his voice startlingly decisive. He was already grabbing his coat and the car keys from the hook by the door. "It's too slow, too exposed. You take the car. Emily's car. It's reliable."

Emily nodded, her face pale but set. She pressed the keys into Jacqueline's hand, then pulled Anna into a final, bone-crushing hug. "You bring our car back," she whispered, a tear slipping down her cheek. "And you bring yourself back."

Two minutes later, they were in the small, blue hatchback, the engine rattling to life. The atmosphere inside was electric with tension. Jacqueline drove, her knuckles white on the wheel, eyes constantly flicking to the mirrors. Anna sat in the back, the lumpy stuffed badger beside her, the real Tulliver a tense, unseen presence in the bag at her feet.

As they left the city sprawl, Tulliver stirred. He produced a carved maple seed, whispered into it, and tossed it from a crack in the window. It unfurled into a winged messenger, darting ahead towards the cottage.

"Sent ahead," Tulliver explained, his voice grim. "Alerting the Grove Warden. A Shaper-class operative has deployed a Weave of Isolation and poisoned a wellspring of the land's strength on the human side. We are returning for tactical reassessment and Veil reinforcement."

Finally, the cottage came into view, a haven of honey-coloured stone in the gathering dusk. Anna looked back one last time, towards London. Closing her eyes for a second, she let her Sight stretch. The distant, golden halo of 'Gentle Bloom' over her home was still there, a tiny beacon. But around it, the feeling of the city was a turbulent, sickly grey, the familiar hum of her street now carrying a new, frightened shiver. The battle had left a scar.

Laylor was waiting at the garden gate, her face grave. Two other fairies hovered behind her, one in the livery of the local Grove, another wearing the severe robes of a Root-Scribe.

"You are expected," Laylor said, her voice taut. "The way is clear. But you must hurry. The forest feels... watched. The Sundered know you are cornered. They will converge here."

There was no time for reunions. No time for tea. This was a military extraction.

Jacqueline grabbed a prepared bag from the cottage door. Anna shouldered her own small pack, her hand brushing the spine of the Locked Chapter book within. Tulliver took point, a glint of something that might have been a tiny, concealed blade appearing in his paw.

"To the Stitch," he said. "Now. Run."

They abandoned the car, the last token of the human world, and plunged into the waiting, silent woods towards the overlapping split in the ancient beech tree.

The blue hatchback sat alone in the lane, the last of the sunset glinting on its windscreen. Inside, the Enchanted Realm, a different kind of war awaited.

CHAPTER 13: The Root–Thorn Covenant

They were not taken to a grand chamber. They were led deep, down, along a root-tunnel that smelled of rich, ancient soil and hummed with a low, sub-audible pulse, the heartbeat of the Great Tree.

The Root-Chamber was a natural vault where colossal roots intertwined like the ribs of a living cathedral. The air was cool and heavy, thrumming with latent power. Bioluminescent fungi and veins of soft, gold Glimmer illuminated the space, revealing the Listener Priestess Elara waiting for them at the chamber's heart. She stood beside the Root-Priest, a timeless figure with skin of polished walnut and hair of fine, white roots.

"The place is prepared," Elara said, her voice the sound of stillness itself. Her pale eyes settled on Anna, and then on the book she carried. "The Primer must be the keystone. Place it within the weave."

Anna stepped forward. In the centre of the chamber, a circle had been prepared on the bare, polished earth. At its cardinal points sat four small bowls. Following Elara's gesture, Anna carefully placed the Locked Chapter, its root-clasp now warm and faintly vibrating, in the very centre.

1. The Weaving of the Place:
Elara and two other acolytes began a low, humming chant. They moved around the circle, sprinkling not just herbs, but substances that represented the layers of the Great Understanding.

Into one bowl, powdered hawthorn wood and London earth.

Into the next, water from the Thames headspring.

Into the third, salt and ash from the cottage hearth.

Into the last, a single, crystallized note from a songbird's call, captured in a drop of resin.

As they chanted, the air within the circle grew still and potent. Anna felt a deep, warm surge from below, the power of the very stone. A cool, silver thread of presence clarified in the air, a path of transition. The space itself seemed to hold its breath, waiting for a story to be sung.

Elara's voice wove names around the sensations, tying the physical offerings to the unseen truths they represented: "The telluric anchor, the foundation, The spirit line, the path of transition,The memory of the hearth, The essence of the songline."

2. The Offering of the Line:
Laylor stepped forward. She placed the lock of Emily's hair into the bowl of earth. "The suffering of the line, acknowledged. The curse's frequency, remembered."
Jacqueline placed a vibrant green leaf from her garden into the water. "The resilience of the line, nurtured by gratitude. The will to grow."
The Root-Priest himself took a single, perfect hawthorn leaf, pricked his thumb with a thorn, and let a drop of his sap-like blood fall onto it. He placed it on Anna's tongue.
"The memory and the duty," he intoned, his voice like roots growing through stone. "Taste the weight of the watch."
Anna's mouth flooded with more than taste, it was knowing. The iron tang of the tree's age, the green burst of life, and the profound, bitter-sweet sorrow of centuries of vigilance. She

felt the root-memory of the Great Hawthorn in Hyde Park, a
sentinel holding back the grey, spiritual pressure of the city.

3. The Binding of the Will & The Unlocking:
"Now," Elara said, her gaze locking with Anna's. "The Primer
is tuned to the truth of your blood. The Locked Chapter was
sealed not by magic, but by ignorance. You have shed that
ignorance. You have listened. Now, understand."
The Root-Priest placed his earth-cool hands on Anna's
temples. "The Tree holds the Law. The blood holds the
Promise. The will must bind them. Do you bind your will to
the Ward of London, to the health of the Veil, to the service
of the Glimmering?"
"I bind my will," Anna said. The words vibrated in the
chamber, absorbed by the humming roots.
"Then receive the Understanding."
The Root-Priest and Elara guided her to her knees. They
pressed her hands, and the hawthorn-marked ankle beneath,
flat against the largest, central root in the chamber.
"Listen."

The world dissolved.

Power, raw and geothermal, shot up from the deepest earth.
It was not a gentle infusion. It was a grafting. Vivid, mossy
roots of emerald light erupted from the great root, wrapping
around her leg, her spine, her consciousness. Sharp,
crystalline thorns of silver spiked from those roots,
anchoring them into her very being, locking her into the vast,
humming network of the world's telluric currents.

And with it came the Great Understanding, coursing up
through the roots and into her mind.

It was not a voice. It was a dimensional shift in perception. She no longer saw the Root-Chamber. She saw the living architecture of Britain. A magnificent, luminous neural network glowed in her vision:

Songlines in threads of gold and memory, weaving stories across the land.

Spirit Lines in cool, quick silver, paths of transition and astral travel.

Telluric Currents in deep, pulsating amber, the continent's lifeblood.

She saw London, a frantic, tangled knot where all three layers were stained and sick, throbbing with a poisonous green frequency. She saw the specific, screaming wound of the allotment. And she saw other, fainter sores, a place in Yorkshire where mirrors drank light wrongly, a silence in Somerset that was not peace, but a void, a museum where history itself was being twisted.

Before her, the Locked Chapter book sprang open. The root-clasp fell away. Knowledge did not pour in as words on a page. It flooded her as direct, intuitive truth. She knew how to stabilize a fraying songline by humming its original tune. She understood how to clear a blocked spirit line by aligning her will with its purpose. She grasped the principle of healing a corrupted telluric node, not by fighting the poison, but by amplifying the land's own immune response, its will to be whole.

The physical mark on her ankle bloomed. The intricate silver filigree of the Ministry Seal transformed. A miniature, perfect hawthorn tree etched itself into her skin, its roots delving deep, its branches reaching up her calf. It glowed with a steady, rooted, green-silver light. It was no longer a brand. It was a living interface, a tuning fork struck true against the heart of the world.

4. The Silence After:
The connection severed as gently as it had begun. The luminous roots and thorns faded from sight, but their presence remained within her, a deep, unshakable foundation. The chamber came back into focus. The chanting had stopped. The book lay open before her, its pages now clear, filled with diagrams of energy flows and resonant frequencies she could read with her soul.

She was the same girl, and yet utterly changed. She was Warden-Apprentice Anna Hawthorne Davis. The roots had recognized her. The thorns had anchored her.

The chamber remained silent for a long, reverent moment. Then, a soft flutter broke the stillness. Laylor landed lightly on the polished earth before Anna, her twilight eyes shimmering with an emotion too deep for simple pride. She reached out and placed a tiny, cool hand on Anna's ankle, just above the living hawthorn mark.

"I have watched over this bloodline from the shadows for decades," Laylor said, her voice a melodic whisper that nonetheless filled the chamber. "I owed a debt to Jacqui, and I paid it in blessings and whispered secrets to the soil. But this ... " She looked up at Anna, her gaze fierce and protective. "This is a new debt. And a new calling."

She turned to face the Root-Priest and Elara, her wings flaring with a sudden, uncharacteristic authority. "The Sundered attacked a human child on my watch, in my realm, because of a debt to *my* name. The corruption they wield now festers in a city I have only glimpsed from the safety of my glade. I will not remain hidden while the consequences of my past walk into battle."

She floated up to Anna's eye level. "You carry the Great Understanding in your bones now, little one. But you do not yet know the faces and follies of the Gentry, the secret languages of the city's hidden kin, or the ways a healer can turn a battlefield into a sanctuary. I will be your guide in the shadows of London, as Elara has been your teacher in the light of the Grove."

The Root-Priest considered this, his ancient face unreadable. "The Glimmering's will is served by those who answer its call. Healer Laylor, you have answered. So let it be woven."

Tulliver, who had been observing from the tunnel's entrance, gave a slow, assessing nod. "A field medic with centuries of experience and a personal stake. Your presence is logical. And welcome."

Laylor turned back to Anna, a gentle smile gracing her lips. "We will face the city's sickness together, Warden-Apprentice. And I will bring us all home."

Elara bowed her head, a minute dip of profound respect. Her work was done.

Anna stood, trembling, the new mark pulsing in time with her heart and the heart of the Tree. The frantic, bird-like fear that had lived in her chest since the allotment was gone. In its place was a deep, rooted calm. Fear was still there, but it was now a surface storm breaking against the mountain of understanding beneath.

Tulliver had not moved. He was staring, utterly still, at the living hawthorn tree on her ankle. He took a slow step closer, circled her once with a tactician's eye, and stopped before her. Then, he inclined his head in a sharp, military gesture of deep, earned respect.

"You are correct," he said, his gravelly voice hushed. "You are anchored. You no longer stand on the earth, Warden-Apprentice. You stand with it. You are part of its will."

He met her eyes, and she saw no trace of the agent babysitting a human child. She saw a veteran looking at a new kind of weapon, one that healed rather than broke.

"The fear is now subordinate," he stated. "Good. That is where it belongs. The power you hold is not a blade to be swung. It is a presence to be wielded. The Sundered break. You must now learn to hold."

He turned toward the tunnel. "Six hours is insufficient. It is also all we have. We will not practice spells. We will practice application. You will trace the sickness in London to its source not by sight, but by resonance. You will feel where the Veil is torn and know how to darn it. The theory is written in your bones. We move to field deployment."

He glanced back, his expression unreadable, but the weight of his gaze was immense. "Do not try to understand it yet. Simply be it. The land will speak. You must answer before the enemy shouts loud enough to drown it out."

Anna understood. The gentle training was over. She was not almost ready.

She was ready. And the wounded, waiting city of London now had a Warden to hear its cry.

CHAPTER 14: THE CALM BEFORE

The world before dawn in the Enchanted Realm was a symphony of hushed tones. Mist clung to the hollows, and the air tasted of cold water and waking earth. In a small, secluded grove, Anna stood barefoot on the moss, her eyes closed.

"Stop trying to listen," Tulliver's voice came from her left, a low rumble in the quiet. He was a shadow in his grey cloak, his new armour making him a solid, blocky silhouette against the pearl-grey light. "You are no longer a listener. You are a participant. What does this place ask of you?"

Anna breathed in, letting the warm, rooted pulse in her ankle expand. She was not an outsider straining to hear a foreign language. She was a note in the chord. The understanding rose effortlessly.

"The stream doesn't just laugh," she said, her voice calm and certain. "Its spirit line is conducting joy. It's a path of pure transition, carrying happiness downstream." She turned her head slightly. "That big oak ... its roots are dreaming in a slow, major key. It's not just old, it's content. Its telluric connection is deep and stable."

"Good. Discernment is passive. Now, interact." Tulliver moved, silent as a shadow. Anna heard the soft click of a small, black pebble being placed on a fern. "There. A splinter of Sundered resonance. It seeks to arrest the local frequency. How does the land wish to respond?"

Anna didn't just feel the pebble's invasive cold. She felt the mild distress of the moss, the subtle recoil of the tiny telluric threads beneath it. The land wished to reject it, to swallow the impurity. She didn't push. She focused through the hawthorn mark, amplifying that natural instinct.

The patch of moss beneath the pebble gave a soft sigh. The black pebble sank, not with violence, but with finality, an inch into the soft earth, as if the ground had quietly closed a minuscule wound.

Tulliver was silent for a long moment. Then he gave a single, slow nod. "Efficient. No wasted energy. You used the land's own rejection mechanism. That is how a Warden operates." His words were no longer instruction, they were a tactical assessment from one professional to another.

Laylor's personal glade was a bowl of sunlight and calm. It smelled of warm honey, chamomile, and crushed herbs.

Anna and Jacqueline sat on a soft tuffet of moss. Jacqueline watched, a soft smile on her face, as Laylor and her two grand-nieces, Bluebell and Copper, flitted about. But her eyes kept returning to Anna. She saw the way the clover leaned towards her niece, not in worship, but in quiet recognition, like sunflowers turning to the sun. She felt it, a deep, steady hum that emanated from Anna, no longer the uncertain spark of potential but the settled resonance of a promise fulfilled. A fierce pride swelled in her chest, edged with the faintest, most loving sorrow: the understanding that Anna was now walking a path where she could no longer lead, only walk beside.

The young fairies were subdued, their wings drooping slightly with remembered shame. But curiosity sparkled in their eyes as they hovered near Anna.

"You're really the Human Warden?" Bluebell whispered, offering a dewdrop in an acorn cup.

"I'm learning to be what that means," Anna said. As she reached for the cup, a nearby patch of forget-me-nots gently turned their blossoms toward the motion.

Copper zipped closer. "Does it hurt? The big tree on your leg?"

Anna showed them the mark. It glowed with its own soft light, the roots seeming to shift subtly under her skin. The fairies gasped in unison.

"It's beautiful," Bluebell breathed. "It looks like ... home."

Laylor settled on a toadstool, her pink-and-green hair vibrant in the sun. "It is more than a picture, little ones," she said, her voice gentle. "She does not carry magic in a pouch. She is a small, walking piece of the Great Understanding. The mark is not a drawing. It is a seed. And where a Warden stands, the world remembers how to be whole." She looked at Anna, her twilight eyes serious. "This is what you are becoming a Warden for, Anna. Not for grand battles in stories, but for the right of glades like this to exist. For the right of my nieces to play tag without fear. You fight for the quiet moments. Never forget that."

Later, as they prepared to leave, Laylor took Jacqueline's hands and placed a small, crystal vial of Heartsease Balm into her palm. The touch was between friends, between equals who shared the same heart if not the same power.

The table in the strategy glade was a living slab of polished burr-wood. Around it sat Tulliver, Laylor, the stern Grove Warden Elmshadow, Anna, and Jacqueline.

Elmshadow laid the magical map of Britain on the table, the three amber pulses glowing ominously. "The tremors have increased. They are probing the Veil like a tongue probing a rotten tooth. The allotment was a test. These are the main events."

He pointed to each pulse. "Yorkshire. Somerset. The London museum. Each is a different type of corrosion."

As he spoke, Anna's gaze lost focus. She wasn't looking at the map, she was feeling the echoes through the root-network now part of her. The Yorkshire signal felt sharp and reflective. The museum pulse was a tangled knot of stolen narratives. But Somerset...

"The Somerset silence," Anna said, her voice cutting softly through Elmshadow's explanation. Everyone turned to her. "It's not just silence. It's a dam."

Elmshadow froze, his twig-like finger hovering over the map. "A dam?"

Anna nodded, her eyes seeing the pressure in her mind. "A major spirit line has been blocked. Not severed. Corked. The emotional and spiritual energy that should flow along it is backing up. Creating pressure. It's not a void, it's a pressure cooker waiting to rupture."

A profound silence filled the glade. Elmshadow's severe face was contemplative. "A dam ... " he mused. "That, aligns with disturbances our water-kin have reported upstream. You can perceive the pressure building?"

"I can feel the strain in the network," Anna confirmed.

Tulliver's gaze, which had been fixed on Anna, shifted to Elmshadow. There was no surprise in his eyes, only grim validation. "If the Warden-Apprentice confirms a structural blockage on a spirit line," he stated, his voice leaving no room for doubt, "then Somerset is not a passive mystery. It is an engineered catastrophe. That changes the tactical priority."

He had used her assessment to reshape their strategic understanding. He had not questioned her. He had built upon her intelligence. Anna felt the weight of the responsibility, and beneath it, the solid foundation of his trust.

The Field Marshal, who had entered silently, leaned over the table, her flint-chip eyes settling on Anna. "Your unit is 'Root & Thorn.' You are the Thorn. Your job is not just to find these sicknesses, but to be the lance that drains them. You leave for London in one hour. Dismissed."

As they stood before the Loose Stitch, the overlapping split in the ancient beech looked different. It wasn't just a doorway, it was a threshold between Anna's two states of being.

They gathered their gear. Tulliver adjusted the strap of his claw-pick. Laylor checked her healer's satchel. Jacqueline pinned the hawthorn sprig over her heart.

Tulliver stopped before the tree. He didn't move to enter first, as was his habit. Instead, he turned his head, his slate-coloured eyes finding Anna.

"Warden-Apprentice," he said, the title deliberate and full. "The Veil is your domain now. You lead the crossing."

It was the ultimate gesture of operational respect. He was ceding the point, the most vulnerable and critical position, to her, acknowledging that her connection to the fabric between worlds surpassed his own.

Anna didn't hesitate. She didn't look to Jacqueline for reassurance. She placed her hand on the warm, humming bark of the tree, feeling the precise frequency of the Veil here, a song only she could hear in its entirety.

She glanced back at her team, her partner, her guardian, her healer. Then she turned sideways, drew in a breath aligned with the glade's spirit line, and stepped through.

The calm was over. The final battle for London's soul awaited its Warden.

CHAPTER 15: THE HOME FRONT

The blue hatchback didn't so much park as siege-break.

Jacqueline wrenched the wheel, sending the car into a skidding halt halfway up the pavement outside 23 Willow Drive. The house stood, but it was wrong. The gentle, golden haze of 'Gentle Bloom' that Anna had seen days before was now a sickly, flickering aurora, straining against an invisible pressure. The air around the terraced row was thick and silent, a dead zone. A sparrow lay frozen on the garden wall, not dead, but caught mid-hop, its tiny life suspended in glue-thick time.

"They're here," Anna breathed, her voice tight. Her hawthorn mark was a thrumming live wire against her ankle. "They've caged the house. Muted the local songline."

In the back seat, Laylor shed her Glamour of insignificance in a ripple of light, her wings a sharp, humming blur. "A Shaper's Weave of Stasis. A subtle knife. It does not cut the body, it suffocates the spirit of a place."

Tulliver was already a solid, grey-clad shape halfway out the door, his claw-pick unslung. "No time for stealth. The guardians are under psychic siege. We break the perimeter. Now."

They moved as a unit. Anna led, her hand outstretched. The oppressive field resisted like cold, dense jelly. She focused, not pushing against it, but re-tuning. She found the shredded remnants of the street's songline, the memory of children playing, of daily comings and goings, and poured her will through her mark, weaving a single, clear note of normalcy back into the silent space.

With a sound like a held breath finally released, the stasis field ruptured. The sparrow completed its hop with a frantic chirp and fled. Noise rushed back, the distant city hum, the wind.

Before they could knock, the front door flew inward. Emily stood there, her face pale, her eyes wide with a fear that wasn't just shock. "The clocks... all the clocks stopped. And the... the quiet." Her gaze darted from Anna to the fully revealed, luminous Laylor and the armored, grim Tulliver. She stumbled back a step.

Jack was behind her, a rolling pin held like a club, his practical face etched with confusion and dread. "Anna? What in God's name"

"No time," Tulliver cut in, striding past them into the hallway, his head on a swivel. "You are under magical assault. The nature of the attack is psychological and spiritual suppression. You are not going mad. You are being silenced."

Jacqueline moved to Emily, taking her hands. "It's the house, Em. They're trying to suffocate its spirit. We're here to make it breathe again."

In the kitchen, the atmosphere was electric with panic and magic. Tulliver didn't ask. He cleared the table with a sweep of his arm and slammed his ironbark scroll-case down. The magical map unrolled, its ley lines glowing, the three amber pulses now glaring like infected wounds.

But something was terribly wrong.

The pulse over the allotment wasn't just glowing, it was convulsing, throbbing in a rapid, erratic rhythm. The pulse over Somerset pulsed in perfect, ominous sync with it.

Anna's breath hitched. She placed her hands flat on the map, closing her eyes. Her consciousness plunged into the root-network, following the agonized threads.

"It's not a breach point anymore," she gasped, her eyes flying open. "It's a pump. They've linked them. The dam in Somerset,the blocked spirit line, they've tapped the pent-up pressure. They're using that bottled emotional energy to supercharge the corruption at the allotment. They're not just probing the Veil, " Her finger stabbed the map, at the converging lines near the centre of London. "They're using the pump to drill. They're looking for the weakest point in the city's spiritual architecture. And they've found it."

Everyone followed her finger. The ley lines twisted like strands of a rope, all tightening towards a single, ancient anchor in the heart of the metropolis.

"The Great Hawthorn in Hyde Park," Laylor whispered, her voice filled with horror. "The sentinel. The heart-ward. They mean to corrupt the anchor itself. If it falls, the Veil over London tears like rotten cloth."

"Then we don't have hours. We have minutes," Tulliver snarled. He looked at Jack and Emily, who were clinging to each other, struggling to comprehend the cosmic disaster unfolding in their kitchen. "You will stay. Inside. The wards on this house are your only shield. Believe in them." He handed Jack the smooth white stone. "If the silence returns, crush this. It is your last shout."

He turned to the team. "Revised objective. We are not intercepting a ritual. We are relieving a besieged fortress. The Hawthorn Tree is the fortress. We move."

As he spoke, the kitchen light began to die.

Not a flicker. A draining. The light from the bulb, from the grey sky at the window, seemed to be leached away, swallowed by a deepening twilight that had no source. The only light left was the angry glow of the map and the soft luminescence of Laylor's form.

Then the sound came. A deep, subsonic HUM that rose from the soles of their feet, vibrating the floorboards, rattling the cups in the cupboard. It was the sound of a colossal, unnatural engine powering up.

Anna's hawthorn mark flared, a spike of pain and warning. She clutched the edge of the table. "The pump ... it's at full power. The drill is active. They've started the final sequence. We're out of time."

No more words. No more plans.

Tulliver snatched up his claw-pick. Laylor's wings became a blade-sharp buzz. Jacqueline grabbed Emily and Jack in one final, crushing hug, then pushed them towards the inner hallway.

Anna was already at the front door. She threw it open.

The world outside was a silent, deepening bruise of purple-black. The streetlights were out. The hum was everywhere, a physical pressure in the chest. And on the horizon, in the direction of Hyde Park, the sky was not dark. It was wrong, a shimmering, sickly vortex of energy, visible only to the Sight, where the world's fabric was being relentlessly ground against a magical drill.

The battle for London hadn't been awaiting its guardians.

It had begun without them.

"To the Tree!" Anna cried, and she led the charge into the humming, lightless street.

CHAPTER 16: THE HEART'S DEFENSE

Hyde Park was dying.

They didn't see it with their eyes at first. They felt it. The very air was thin, sucked of vitality. The cheerful, tangled songline of Londoners at leisure, children laughing, couples strolling, the memory of a thousand sunny days, was frayed to a desperate, fading whisper.

And at its centre stood the Great Hawthorn Tree. Or what was left of it.

A column of sickly, pulsating green energy, the "drill" from the linked corruption of Somerset and the allotment, bore directly into its gnarled trunk. The Tree's usual aura of steadfast, gentle power was contorted, its natural silver-green light fighting a losing battle against the invasive poison. Leaves, out of season, browned and fell in a silent, continuous rain.

Anna's gasp was one of physical pain. The assault wasn't just on her senses, it was in her bones, transmitted through the root-network she was now part of. The Tree's agony was a shriek of splintering wood and silenced birdsong that only she could hear fully.

"They're not just attacking it," she choked out, staggering, her hand pressed to her blazing hawthorn mark. "They're … inverting it. They're using the drill to re-write its resonance. Turning its own anchoring power against the Veil. If they finish the Veil won't tear. It will unravel from here. A slow, unstoppable un-knitting of reality."

Laylor let out a soft cry of despair. Tulliver's face was carved from the same stone as his armour. "A cascade failure. Their objective was never a spectacle. It was an extinction."

"We have to stop the focus," Anna said, forcing her mind to work through the pain. She plunged her awareness deeper into the network, tracing the malignant algorithm of the spell. "The inversion needs a living conductor to complete the final sequence. Krawl has to physically touch the Tree at the focal point of that beam."

Tulliver's slate eyes gleamed with instant, ruthless calculus. "Then we do not stop the beam. We use it. We make the Tree seem to falter. We draw the conductor in. And we snap the trap shut on him."

The Bait

They moved with the precision of a trap-setting predator.

Laylor flew to the base of the Tree. Instead of fighting the corruption directly, she let her healing magic flicker and dim. To any observer, especially one tuned to Glimmer-frequencies, it would look like a healer's last, failing effort. She allowed a patch of bark under the beam to darken visibly.

Jacqueline knelt, driving her hands into the cold London soil. She couldn't speak to it like the soil of her garden, but she could shout with her intent. She sent pulses of simulated distress, waves of fear, weakness, and root-deep fatigue, rippling through the local telluric current. The ground itself seemed to sigh and weaken.

Anna stood back, her eyes closed, weaving the final part of the illusion. She gently damped the Tree's own defiant songline, making its struggle seem quieter, further away. To Krawl, it would smell like blood in the water.

"He will come," she whispered.

The Brawl

He did not walk. He precipitated.

From the roiling corruption of the drill-beam, from the miasma of dead leaves and despair, his form drew together. This was Krawl at the peak of his stolen power. He was larger, his form a jagged cathedral of soot, rust, and shattered tile, the green lights in his eye-sockets blazing like toxic stars. The hum of the drill seemed to sync with the grinding of his joints.

"The heart weakens," his voice grated, the sound of a city's foundations cracking. "The guardian's light gutters. I will be the final stroke. The silence after the scream." He ignored the small figures at the Tree's base. His prize was within reach.

"Not today."

Tulliver stepped into his path. No glamour. No stuffed toy. This was Field Agent Tulliver, First Cohort of the Accord's Guard, in his full battle regalia. Ironbark plates, etched with faint protective runes, covered him from neck to paw, gleaming dully in the corrupted light. His grey cloak was thrown back. In his hands, his claw-pick was not a tool, but a spear.

Krawl swung a limb of conglomerate rubble. Tulliver was not there. He was a blur of grey, a low spin bringing his pick around to score a deep, sizzling furrow along Krawl's leg. "You are slow," Tulliver rasped. "You are a symptom. I am the cure."

The fight was brutal, a clash of opposites. Krawl was raw, overwhelming power, shockwaves of force, lashing tendrils of corrupted shadow, blasts of chilling energy. Tulliver was precision, speed, and an unbreakable will. He deflected, dodged, and struck like a viper, each hit aimed at a joint, a glowing seam, a point of structural weakness.

But he was one against a force of nature. A backhanded blow caught him, sending him skidding across the frost-bitten grass, his armour screeching. He rose, a crack in one shoulder plate, but his grip on his weapon was steady.

"Hey, slag-heap!" Jacqueline's voice cut through the din. She hurled a small satchel Laylor had given her. It burst against Krawl's back in a cloud of purifying salt and ground hawthorn bark. Where it stuck, his form sizzled and smoked. He roared, turning his fury on her.

It was the distraction Tulliver needed. He lunged, driving his claw-pick deep into the juncture of what passed for Krawl's hip. The creature bellowed, a sound of grinding machinery, and flung Tulliver away with a blast of concussive force. The agent hit the ground hard, this time struggling to rise, one arm hanging limp.

Krawl, limping but triumphant, turned back to the Hawthorn. The path was clear. The Tree seemed to wilt before him. He raised a clawed hand, dripping with condensed malice, reaching for the dark patch on the bark, the final connection.

The Warden's Gambit

"You're not touching my city's heart."

Anna stepped from the shadows of the great roots. She was not hiding. She was centred. Her hands were flat on the living bark of the Hawthorn, her forehead resting against it. The hawthorn mark on her ankle blazed so brightly it cast her own long shadow. The air around her hummed with a different frequency, not the drill' scream, but the deep, patient, root-song of the world.

Krawl's green eyes flared. "The little root. The would-be Warden. You are too late."

"No," Anna said, her voice echoing with a resonance not her own. "You are exactly on time."

She slammed her will not against the drill, but through the Tree, into the prepared root-code she had woven during the illusion. She did not attack Krawl.

She invited him in.

The ground at his feet erupted. Not with crushing roots, but with living filaments of silver and green, pure, concentrated Glimmer shaped by the Great Understanding. They did not pierce. They wove. They snaked around his limbs, his torso, following the chaotic, screaming frequency of his own corruption and, stitch by psychic stitch, began to re-knit it into harmony.

It was an agony of order. Krawl screamed, a sound of pure, undiluted horror, as the entropy that defined him was forcibly stabilized, organized, and solidified. He was trapped in a cocoon of scintillating light, his form rigid, his malevolent will battling the relentless, peaceful logic of the binding.

Tulliver limped to his feet, standing tall beside Jacqueline. Laylor floated forward, her face stern. They formed a circle around the seething, light-wrapped form.

"Krawl, agent of the Sundered," Tulliver intoned, his voice the dry, unforgiving rasp of the law. "By the authority of the Root-Script and the Ministry Accords, you are adjudged guilty of attempted Veilicide and corruption of a sentinel. Your sentence is the Gargoyle Pact."

Laylor raised her hands, her healing magic flowing not to mend, but to set. To make the transformation permanent, cellular, absolute.

Jacqueline poured her will into the circle, the fierce, protective love of a guardian, the unyielding desire for a safe and growing world.

Anna channeled it all. She was the conduit. She looked at the monster in the light, feeling its rage, its nihilism, its absolute loneliness. And she showed it, through the binding, what it had tried to destroy. Not an image, but a truth: the quiet joy of her aunt's garden, the laughter of Laylor's nieces, the steadfast resilience of the Hawthorn Tree, the million fragile, beautiful connections of the Glimmering world.

"You sought to break the Veil," Anna said, the words final and heavy as mountains. "Now, you will guard it. You sought to spread decay. Now, you will be stone, impervious. Your consciousness will remain. A witness. A sentinel. Forever."

With a sound like a distant bell and a closing vault, the light crystallized.

The shimmering cocoon hardened, greyed, and reshaped. The filaments became weathered wing-feathers, the binding vines transformed into twisted stone limbs. Where Krawl had been, there now crouched a grotesque, powerfully built statue of a winged beast, its muzzle frozen in a silent snarl, its empty eye-sockets staring eternally outward over the park. It radiated a cold, immovable stillness.

Above it, the corrupting drill-beam flickered, cracked, and shattered into harmless motes of fading light.

The silence that followed was profound. It was the silence after a storm. The ordinary, blessed sounds of the city at night rushed back in, the distant sigh of traffic, the wind in the real, unharmed branches of the Hawthorn Tree, the call of a lone bird reclaiming its park.

The Great Hawthorn Tree gave a gentle shudder. Its leaves stopped falling. Its bark, where the dark patch had been, began to glow again with its own, soft, silver-green light. The un-knitting had been stopped. The heart of London beat on.

Anna sank to her knees, exhausted, the light fading from her mark to its usual warm pulse. She was spent, but the rooted calm within her was unbroken. They had done it.

Tulliver placed a firm, careful paw on her shoulder. No words. None were needed. Jacqueline and Laylor gathered close, a circle of weary, triumphant guardians around their Warden, in the shadow of the Tree they had saved.

CHAPTER 17: ROOT & THORN

The silence in Anna's old bedroom at 23 Willow Drive was the good kind. It was the silence after a storm has passed, leaving behind clean, calm air. Sunlight, real and ordinary, streamed through the window.

Anna lay on her bed, staring at the familiar ceiling cracks. The hawthorn mark on her ankle was a warm, steady presence, like a loyal dog sleeping at her feet. Down the hall, she could hear the low murmur of her parents talking with Jacqueline in the kitchen, the clink of mugs, a soundscape of peaceful normality she thought this house had forgotten how to make.

They had arrived here last night, a weary, victorious procession emerging from the hushed park into the returning London noise. Her parents had met them at the door, their faces etched with a day of worry that melted into bewildered relief at the sight of their daughter, her aunt, and their two extraordinary companions.

There had been explanations, of a sort. "A nasty gas leak near the park," Tulliver had stated with such bland authority it sounded like gospel. "Caused mass hallucinations. We got caught in it. All clear now." It was a thin story, but it was a story, and her parents, living in the joyful haze of their own reversed fortunes, were inclined to believe in happy endings.

Now, in the morning light, Anna could see the truth of it. The 'Gentle Bloom' enchantment wasn't a flickering shield anymore. It was woven in, a gentle, golden permanence in the very bricks of the house, in the shine of her mother's eyes, in the relaxed set of her father's shoulders. The curse was gone. Not broken, but transmuted. Its energy had been recycled into this durable, quiet luck. Her family's battlefield was now a sanctuary, permanently warded by the Ministry's gratitude.

The hidden entrance to the Bureau outpost was behind a shelf of crumbling law books in a musty shop on Cecil Court. Tulliver triggered it with a tap of a claw, and they descended a narrow spiral staircase into a room that smelled of ozone and old stone.

The severe Ministry official was waiting, his living scroll casting a cool light on his impassive face. But his first words were not of procedure.

"The Great Hawthorn is stable," he said. "Its songline is purging the last of the corruption. London's heart-ward holds." His gaze swept over them, lingering on Anna. "Your actions prevented a cascade failure. This is noted."

He moved on, all business, unrolling the map of Britain across the table. Its surface still showed the faint, faded echoes of where the three glowing sores had been, Yorkshire, Somerset, the museum, but they were little more than ghost-images now, scars already healing.

"The threat is neutralized," the official stated. "The Sundered network in Britain has suffered a critical collapse. Without Krawl as their anchor and the Hawthorn's corruption reversed, their remaining operations are ... disorganized. Fleeing. Hiding." He looked up, his ancient eyes meeting Anna's. "You closed the wound. The Veil will mend the rest."

Anna placed her hand on the map, letting her senses drift. She felt it, the slow, patient return of health. The Yorkshire mirrors, once a sharp, reflective wrongness, were now just strange antiques gathering dust in empty rooms. The Somerset silence had unblocked, she could almost hear the distant, joyful rush of a spirit line flowing freely again. And the museum ... the museum's tangled stories were untangling themselves, the stolen narratives finding their way back to their rightful places in the earth.

It was done.

"The operational designation for your unit is now formal," the official continued, rolling the map away. "Task Force: Root & Thorn. You are a scalpel that has proven its edge. But for now?" A flicker of something almost like warmth crossed his severe face. "For now, you rest. You heal. You tend your own roots. When, *if*, the Glimmering calls you again, it will find you ready."

Tulliver gave a sharp nod, accepting the dismissal without question. No strategic debate. No talk of where they would go next.

Anna understood. This wasn't a pause between missions. This was an ending. A real one.

The official's gaze settled on her one last time. "You are dismissed, Warden. All of you. Go home."

The train ride back to the countryside was a liminal space. They had a compartment to themselves. Laylor was a small, luminous blur by the window, watching the world streak past. Tulliver studied the Yorkshire file, his brow furrowed. Jacqueline dozed, her head against the glass. Anna sat, feeling the hum of the tracks through the soles of her shoes, a mundane rhythm that soothed her spirit.

They arrived as the late afternoon sun was painting the hills in gold. The cottage, with its honey-coloured stone and wild roses, appeared at the end of the lane like a promise kept.

It was only there, in the deepening twilight of the garden, that the final weight lifted.

Laylor hovered before Jacqueline, touching the mark over her heart. "A mark of partnership," she whispered, and the vine-tracery glowed, a new leaf unfurling in its design. The debt was gone. What remained was choice.

Tulliver stood beside Anna at the garden's edge, looking toward the woods. "We have a pact," he stated, his voice gravelly but clear. "My tactics. Your sight. We are stronger together. That is the bond that matters."

"Partner," Anna said.

He gave a single, grunting nod.

Then Anna looked at Jacqueline, and her aunt looked back. They each placed a hand over their marks, ankle and heart. A warm, silent pulse passed between them, a heartbeat that said, Here. Safe.

No more words were needed. They were Root & Thorn. The persistent, growing thing. A family forged in magic and choice.

Later, in the warm, lamplit kitchen, Jacqueline placed four mugs of cocoa on the worn table. "Right then," she said, her smile deep and sure. "Yorkshire. When do we leave?"

Anna wrapped her hands around her mug, feeling the warmth seep into her bones. She looked around at her healer, her guardian, her warrior. She felt the rooted pulse of her mark, connecting her to the quiet, singing heart of the world.

She was home. And her home was now this team, this duty, this vast, secret world she was sworn to protect.

"Soon," Anna said, her voice calm with certainty. "The Veil will tell us when."

Outside, the first stars appeared over the cottage, and in the dark line of the woods, the Loose Stitch waited, a silent gateway to the next adventure.

Later that night, long after Jacqueline had gone to bed, Anna sat alone in the moonlit garden. The hawthorn mark on her ankle pulsed with a quiet, satisfied rhythm, in tune with the sleeping flowers and the distant hum of the woods. The battle for London was over. Her family was safe, permanently warded. Her team, Root & Thorn, was bonded. For the first time in weeks, the knot in her chest was completely, utterly gone.

A perfect, peaceful silence.

Then, she felt it.

It wasn't a sound. It wasn't a vision. It was a *pull*. A deep, ancient, irresistible tugging sensation that seemed to come from somewhere far below the warm, familiar pulse of the Glimmer, from the very bones of the earth.

Her mark flared, not in warning, but in something like awe. It was a frequency so old, so primal, it made the Great Tree feel like a sapling. It was the smell of dark stone and the first rain on volcanic rock. It was the memory of a world before words, before fairies, before the Veil itself.

And with it came a single, terrifying, and exhilarating certainty: *There is something deeper.*

Anna's breath caught. She stood, her eyes fixed on the ground beneath her feet as if she could see through it to the planet's core. The pull was gentle, but insistent. It wasn't a threat. It was an invitation. A question from a place so old it had forgotten how to speak in anything but feeling.

Who walks above? Will you remember us? Will you come down?

She didn't answer. Not yet. She didn't even know how. But as the feeling faded, leaving only the quiet hum of the garden in its wake, Anna knew one thing with absolute clarity.

The war in London was won. The problems of this realm were resolved. But her journey as a Warden was not over.

It was only just beginning.

And the next call would come from somewhere no book in Aunt Jacq's library had ever described.

[End of Book One]

About the Author

Robin Parker began his writing journey after a fulfilling career nurturing young minds as a teacher. At sixty-five, he traded lesson plans for story outlines, drawing on his Bachelor's degree in Education and Diploma in Early Learning to craft stories shaped by wonder, curiosity, and a lifelong love of the natural world. He believes, deeply, that imagination does not retire.

Writing from a cosy corner of New South Wales, Australia, Robin now devotes his time to building layered worlds and memorable characters. His debut novel, Zytopra: The Divine Cat, introduced readers to a banished feline god determined to reclaim his lost dominion. He later stepped into the world of children's literature with Welcome to Bluegum Hill, a gentle picture book celebrating Australian bush animals and early discovery.

With The Warden-Apprentice and the Saundered War: Root and Thorn, Robin continues to expand his epic fantasy universe, exploring loyalty, power, sacrifice, and the deep-rooted bonds that shape destiny.

Robin writes with the conviction that some of life's greatest adventures begin exactly when we least expect them.

You've finished the story... but the world continues.

Thank you for journeying through The Warden-Apprentice and the Saundered War: Root and Thorn.

As a reader, you are invited to a private page created especially for you. There you'll discover:

- A free Companion Pack

- A bonus chapter

- A free ebook

- Exclusive updates on the next instalment

This is my way of saying thank you, and of keeping you close to the story as it grows.

Scan the QR code or visit the link below to continue the adventure.

Also by Robin Parker

Zytopra: The Divine Cat

A god betrayed. A mortal reborn. A divine reckoning
begins.

Three thousand years ago, Zytopra was worshipped
as a god. Betrayed by those he trusted, his divinity
was stripped away, and he was condemned to live
again and again as a mortal.

Now reborn as a black cat in the modern world,
Zytopra remembers everything. When he chooses a
quiet young girl as his priestess, he begins the slow
work of rebuilding his power , not through temples
and armies, but through patience, influence, and
quiet acts of protection.

Zytopra: The Divine Cat is a myth-inspired fantasy
about exile, loyalty, and the long game of justice,
told through the eyes of a god who has learned that
true power does not always announce itself.

robindparker.com

www.ingramcontent.com/pod-product-compliance
Lightning Source LLC
Chambersburg PA
CBHW031309060726
47590CB00003B/1121